Madam President and the Admiral

11/21/08

To my classmate Perry:

Smooth Sailing.

Carl Nel

Carl Nelson

A sequel to the award winning novel *Secret Players*

Copyright 2008© by Carl Nelson
Library of Congress Number
ISBN 978-1-890035-66-2

Published by
New Century Press
1055 Bay Blvd., Suite C
Chula Vista, CA 91911
800 519-2465
www.newcenturypress.com

Other books by Carl Nelson

FICTION

- *Secret Players*
- *The Advisor (Có-ván)*

NON-FICTION

- *Your Own Import-Export Business: Winning the Trade Game*
- *Import/Export: How to Get Started in International Trade*
- *Global Success: International Business Tactics of the 1990s*
- *Managing Globally: A Complete Guide to Competing Worldwide*
- *International Business: A Manager's Guide to Strategy in the Age of Globalism*
- *Exporting: A Manager's Guide to World Markets*
- *Protocol for Profit: A Manager's Guide to Competing Worldwide*

Acknowledgments

Many very nice folks added their ideas and assistance to bring this book to market including my wife Dolores Hansen Nelson, Linda Carter, Tricia Van Dockum, and Greg Smith. For their help, I am grateful.

Warmest Regards,
Carl Nelson
www.carl-a-nelson.com

Prologue

Abigail Cass Steele is a descendant of one of the most respected Michigan families. Her great-great-grandfather, Lewis Cass, had been the first governor of the Michigan Territory and started CASS Company, a small lumber firm.

When Buck Steele, a brash World War II hero and Abby's eventual husband, came to Saginaw, he took the helm of CASS Company and turned it into America's first conglomerate. Later, when the corporation had serious financial issues, Abby took over the reins as president and CEO of CASS Corporation.

Abby's brother, Harmon "Pud" Cass III, chose the path of his grandfather and moved quickly up the political ladder. After a strenuous campaign, Pud won the election for President of the United States. Pud asked Buck to act as special envoy for a serious negotiation with Japan. When Buck suffered a heart attack and died, Abby, out of necessity, took over negotiations. Proving her worth against the Japanese set her course into the political arena.

Against considerable political opposition, Pud appointed Abby as his Secretary of State. During the third year of his presidency, Pud was diagnosed with lung cancer and died.

Already well known for her shrewd grit and astute understanding of the political process, Abby campaigned vigorously in the next election for the Michigan senatorial seat and won hands down.

During Abby's second term in office, her party drafted her at the national convention to run for president. She took on the campaign with fervor and made speeches that set all eyes upon her.

An excerpt in a national newspaper recounted one of her primary beliefs with the winning phrase: "I will adhere to our nation's founding principles and defend the freedom of the American people."

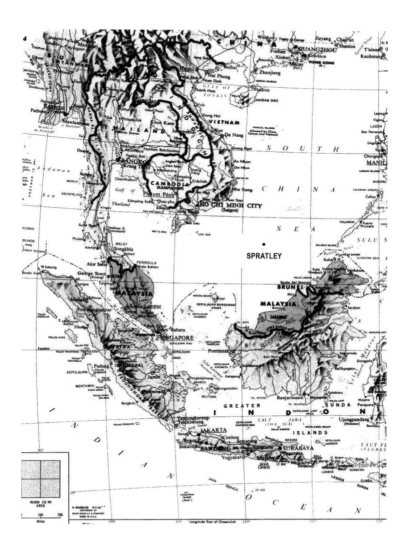

~ **One** ~

"How do you know if there's a fighter pilot at your party?" Skinhead asked as he scanned his gauges and the placid horizon ahead.

"Got me, skipper," His co-pilot, Lieutenant Roger "Jelly" Bean answered.

"He'll tell you."

"Good one." Jelly laughed. "Real good. Okay, okay. Here's one for you, Skinhead. What's the difference between God and fighter pilots?"

"Heard it before," Skinhead replied. "God doesn't think he's a fighter pilot."

"Okay, okay, try this one," Jelly said. "What's the difference between a fighter pilot and a jet engine?"

"Got me."

"A jet engine stops whining when the plane shuts down."

Looking over his shoulder to the compartment behind him, Skinhead said into his lip mike, "Hey, Money. Check your nav — you sure we're only a hundred out from the Spratlys?"

"Roger, checking." Lieutenant Junior Grade Miller Bonds reached for the satellite gear. His eyes scanned the readout. Then he looked at the chart on the table in front of him.

Lieutenant Bill "Skinhead" Smalley, the pilot of a Navy surveillance aircraft, had a mission to survey what was happening around the Spratly Islands.

During preflight Skinhead learned that this small group of coral reefs and islands had served as a Japanese submarine base during World War II but that recent discoveries showed abundant oil and natural gas deposits. The pre-flight briefer warned Skinhead, "A Chinese naval force might be in the vicinity ready to take possession of the islands by force — be careful."

"How far are we from the nearest land?" Skinhead asked.

"Three hundred miles as the crow flies from Vietnam, about the same from Brunei and Malaysia."

"Like, we *are* the crows. We should be outside fighter range — like, what're those J-10's doing here?" Skinhead pointed out the starboard cockpit window.

Next to Lieutenant Smalley's plane, in tight formation, flew two J-10 fighters, the best the Chinese military had. "Shit, Jelly. Shouldn't we have had a heads-up from our AWACS?"

"They didn't come from a land base, unless they were tanked," Jelly said.

"Details, baby. They're here. The Chinese navy's out here. That's all that counts," Skinhead said. "Better make the call. No tell'n what those assholes'll do."

"Roger. Switching," Jelly said. "This is Beacon 3, Tangle Up, I say again Tangle Up." He looked at Skinhead. "Sent. What're you gonna do?"

"Hey... what we were sent out here to do. Check out the fuckin' Spratly Islands."

"Don't think those two agree — Chinese navy found us first. They're trying to turn us."

"Fuck'em. Sail on. I'm headin' for the deck. Hang on, baby!" Skinhead pushed the nose of his plane in the direction of the ocean below and throttled back to a speed the fighters would find hard to match.

"Skinhead! That was a missile that just passed us. The bastards let one fly."

The American pilots watched the burst of flame from the tail of what they hoped was an unarmed rocket as it flew by and continued into the space ahead.

"Call it in."

"Roger." Jelly switched channels. "This is Beacon 3, Tangle Tangle, I say again, Tangle Tangle." To Skinhead: "I hope there's some help around. Like a squadron of fighter jocks! Where are they when we need 'em?"

"Hey! We're hit! Hang on, we're go'n in!"

~ Two ~

Military Aide-de-camp Commander Betty Porter, rushed through the Oval Office door, "Ma'am, Chinese jets just shot down one of our planes."

"Is our crew alive?" asked President Abigail Cass Steele.

"Don't know, ma'am," replied the tense voice in the lingering patois of her early years in Harlem, "But they need you in the Situation Room right away."

"Let's go, Betty."

Two stick-straight Marines stood at the entrance to one of the most secure places in the White House, soundproofed and debugged daily. They both saluted, but only one shouted, "Attention on deck. The President of the United States."

After Abby took her place, seventeen other somber-faced men and women took their seats at the long table. Several staffers lined a back row against the wall.

"Is our crew alive?" Abby asked.

"We don't know, ma'am," Defense Secretary Read Alseño responded. Young, nattily dressed with a Hollywood look, he was picked for his job from the California defense industry.

"What happened?"

Alseño rose to stand by a digitized techno-plasma screen. One end showed a map of the world, color-dotted with spots of hot activity.

"Two Chinese JH-10A fighters jumped one of our multi-mission maritime aircraft on a routine recon mission near the Spratly Islands. As we speak, there's an amphibious group, here..." He pointed to the waters southeast of Asia. "...The Phib Group Commander sent Marine aircraft to conduct a search and rescue mission."

"If there are casualties, I'll call the families," the president said.

"The president doesn't personally notify them," Chairman of the Joint Chiefs Contract Mullin said bluntly. "We take care of that."

"I may wish to handle it personally," she said in a quiet, level tone showing that same short-lipped smile that endeared her to her constituency. It disguised her recognition that Mullin had just talked down to her.

"Yes, ma'am." His made-for-radio face stoically covered any sense of embarrassment.

"How do we know they were Chinese fighters?" she asked.

"Smalley got off a report before we lost contact."

"Smalley is?"

"Lieutenant Bill Smalley, the pilot of the MMA."

"Air Force or Navy?"

"Navy."

5

"Hmm, Spratlys?"

Secretary Alseño pointed to a tiny speck on the Asian chart. "You may recall from your days at the Senate that the Spratlys are a group of very small islands, really no more than a bunch of coral reefs and sandbars, here in the South China Sea. They're about equidistant from the surrounding landmasses. Because of the discovery of oil fields there, just about every country in the vicinity lays claim to them: China, Malaysia, the Philippines, Vietnam, even the nationalists of Taiwan."

"I don't see a 'hot-spot' marked on that map," she said.

"This attack jumped out of nowhere, ma'am."

"Why would they shoot down our plane? The United States and the Peoples Republic of China haven't been at odds since President Nixon opened a dialog in the mid '70s. We're still on good terms with them, except for the continuing problem over the island of Taiwan."

General Mullin, whose body shape matched his nickname "Bull," leaned forward. "Because there's something they haven't wanted us to see."

"So they just shot it down?" She frowned. "Was it a mistake? Something similar happened back in the '90s. Answer my question, please. Why?"

"Madam President," Mullin's brusque tone changed to one of condescension. "We had intel a

Chinese naval force was on the move near the Spratlys. We sent our planes to check it out."

"What intel?"

"You want the whole story?" Secretary Alseño asked.

"Of course." She motioned her hands in exasperation.

"You're up, Napoleon." Alseño glanced in the direction of a short, black-haired man with a Roman nose.

Director of Intelligence Sam Talau acquired his nickname long ago due to his aggressive style, knowing all the angles, a CIA man who actually participated in secret warfare. At five foot four, dressed in his Brooks Brothers blue suit and wing-tipped shoes, he tended to have a little-boy look, incapable of being mean or dangerous. But his cauliflower ears and lack of any discernable neck appeared to be obvious products of being a wrestler in his college days at Annapolis.

Abby thought, *anyone really acquainted with Sam should never, ever underestimate him.*

Sam scrambled to a position in front of the world map. He broke into a grin and barked as if still in the Marine Corps. "My briefing is at our highest security level. Everyone without special clearance must leave."

Abby nodded agreement and waited, dignified and erect. She wore a simple dark gray dress. Her scarf, twisted casually around her throat and secured by a broach, had a splash of vivid red surrounded by pastel colors that blended with her stylishly coiffured auburn hair. Her folded hands rested near the edge of the table. Besides a small watch, her only piece of jewelry was a bracelet on her right wrist, a gift from Buck, her deceased husband.

The muffled noise of shuffling bodies fell across the room. Back-rowers, second-level staffers, even two cabinet members picked up their papers and left.

With the door secured behind them and the lights softened to accommodate a visual presentation, Sam said, "President Steele, when you're ready." He waited respectfully for her signal.

She nodded.

"Only last week Premier Sun Yuxi made an observation about their country," he opened. "I quote, 'In terms of per capita income and gross national product, China is now a 'first world' country. Our people deserve respect.' The premier went on to say, 'Contrary to articles published in the *Washington Post* and *London Times*, China has only peaceful intentions. We expand our influence only to obtain oil to satisfy the nation's shortages.'"

"That, Madam President," Sam continued, "excuse my French, but that's bullshit. The operative word here is *expand*. The CIA is *not* getting much intelligence out of China. And the ambassador's team hasn't been much help either, but we believe the Chinese are on the move. We know they ordered a large naval force into the South China Sea. We think it's in anticipation of their border dispute with the Russians. We also believe taking possession of the Spratlys will be their first step, but only a first step. If Russia moves to take over the Chinese Pan-Asian pipeline, they'll go to war with Russia."

"What's this about an oil pipeline?" Abby asked.

"It stretches from here," Sam pointed. "Kazakhstan on the Caspian Sea, across Uzbekistan and Tajikistan into the northern tip of China. And that's the problem. Russia claims that spit of land."

"Why am I just learning about a potential conflict here?"

Secretary Alseño turned quickly in his chair. "Because until now it's been below the radar. Probably didn't get the attention it deserved during the transition. We thought it was just another of several border problems in the world."

"Why are we not getting better intelligence?" she asked.

"China's gone silent, ma'am," Sam interjected. "We can't get anyone of any consequence in the government to talk."

"Wilmer, what do you hear from our ambassador?" She directed her eyes to Secretary of State Wilmer Flanagan, the slender, lined-faced, elder statesman of her cabinet, sitting opposite Alseño.

"Frankly, Madam President, not much. He agrees the Chinese are unusually quiet."

"How do we know they have a naval force in the South China Sea?"

"Satellite," Alseño answered.

"Continue with your brief, Sam," she said.

"Yes, ma'am. As I said, if the Chinese go to war with Russia, we think they'll use that as an excuse to take control of oil supplies — divert the super tankers that sail from the Persian Gulf through the Indian Ocean. We also think they're trying to cut a deal with the Saudis to monopolize Middle East oil."

"What are we doing now?" Abby sat forward. "Rather, what should we do?"

"It means we're on the edge of war, right, general?" Alseño smiled toward the chairman of the Joint Chiefs.

"Right, boss," responded Mullin. "Not just on the edge, this is it. A hot war situation. Of course, the Taiwan problem still exists. The PRC'll probably jump on that one as part of their expansion. They'll invade Taiwan. They shot down one of our planes, ma'am. That's an attack on America. It's the beginning. I jus' think you gotta move quickly. Declare war. Don't let them take the Spratlys. Retaliate... Roosevelt did it when a German sub tried to torpedo one of our destroyers in the Atlantic and again when the Japs attacked Pearl. President Johnson did it when a ship was attacked in the Tonkin Gulf. Kennedy almost did it with Cuba and the Russians. Hell, send the fleet out there with some Marines. Drive them back. Kick their butts. We gotta do somethin'. Let 'em sumbitches know we mean business. Don't you agree, Madam President?"

Bull's sneer, the tone, and the overkill approach touched a nerve. She felt he goaded her and compared her to the former male presidents.

"Go to war immediately? Attack them?" She looked about the table. "Do you all agree?" Some heads nodded. The eyes of others dipped toward the direction of their shoes.

Why would Bull push a declaration of war? And why no disagreement around the table? Is it because he has the military voice and they don't want to cross him so early in the administration? I think the Chinese and my top military man just blind-sided me.

"War has always been a last resort for this country, general." Her smile retracted. "I'll decide if or when we go to war."

"Of course, Madam President, but mark my words," Mullin warned with the same condescending tone. "We will have to fight the Chinese sooner or later."

She squinted, her jaw tightened. "You may be right, but if you're wrong, we could start World War Three."

"Let me play this back," President Cass said as she scanned her advisors. "Russia and China are poised to fight over a border dispute and an oil pipeline. If war breaks out, they will need to replace that oil. They expand by taking the Spratly Islands, then take control of the mid-East oil trade route and risk a world war? China fights Russia and takes us and Taiwan on at the same time? None of it makes sense." She took a deep breath. "I have followed China and this is out of character. For goodness sake, China was our ally during WWII, granted before the Chicoms and Mao, when we dealt with a bunch of warlords. But the Chinese people must remember. This could be about oil or property, or both, but my take is it's about something else. Something we've never faced before. As commander-in-chief, I will decide."

"What about the DEFCON — Defense Condition?" Bull asked.

"What about it, general?"

"I recommend upping it, ma'am."

"No. Before we get all Ramboed up, I need to know a lot more. Ladies and gentlemen, we need intelligence — ASAP. I need options."

~ **Three** ~

When Abby returned to her father's old desk she'd brought from her hometown of Saginaw, a thought crossed her mind. Have I read Bull Mullin wrong? True, he is my appointee. Maybe he slipped through the screening process. He came to the job of chairman from Chief of Staff of the Army, chosen because we thought he was the anathema of the previous administration.

Although I'm not paranoid by nature, the methods of Washington politics are not lost on me. D.C. people have their own agendas. This could be an ambush by the previous administration. The media called them a bunch of behind-the-scenes elitists and warmongers. Known also as a band of white male strata dwellers, they tried to dictate how the world should be run. I suspect many of them have overly-negative feelings about a woman being President.

I knew Mullin from my days as a senator, the son of a southern senator with a West Point degree. He'd punched the right operational jobs but spent most of his career in Washington. He wears the trappings of America's wars on his chest, a world I know little about, yet I am the commander-in-chief and Bull Mullin's boss.

"Well," she said aloud. "As they say back in Michigan, 'the frost is off the rose.'"

Glancing at her watch she realized she had enough time to pen a note to her granddaughter before dressing for the evening state dinner. Nicknamed as the third Anna in the family, "Third," was a senior at Barnard. Her picture sat on the president's desk alongside those of Third's brothers, who had equally strange nicknames: "Muscle" and "Bone". An early photo of Abby's deceased husband Buck showed him with his arms around their daughter Anna and son Richard. Her hand touched another photo of her companion and confidant, Admiral Blake Lawrence, now retired after a long career in command of Navy forces.

After signing the letter to Third, Abby leaned back in her chair and idly stroked Whisper, her twelve-year-old tabby cat. She drew a deep breath and closed her eyes, savoring the pleasant scent of cherry blossoms that floated across the Potomac River on an early spring breeze.

With Whisper cradled in her arms, she rose to cross the room to the open window that framed the rose garden and the panoply of federal buildings beyond.

How am I going to serve this country? I have the office for four years.

She thought of Arlington National Cemetery where the body of her late husband lay at rest with other men and women who had served America. *I'm still in awe of this place and its responsibilities — it rests heavily — the capitol city — the people's house.*

She stroked Whisper while her thoughts flowed. What concerns me is what former presidents might think about me, a woman — not the presidents of the second half of the twentieth century like Ike or Jimmy or Ronnie, but men like George Washington or Thomas Jefferson or even Abe or Teddy. Would they think me too soft with too many feelings or want me to be a bitch? They might not have wanted a woman president, ever.

On the other hand, being good at anything in this man's world is difficult, let alone being a woman. Not that I haven't had my share of successes. All eyes are upon me, many wishing I'll fail. But the voters must want me to be different or why else elect a woman?

Abby set Whisper on the floor and watched as the cat wandered off. *Ah, for the life of a feline — to walk away so casually.*

~ **Four** ~

A Marine loudly announced, "Ladies and gentlemen, the President of the United States accompanied by Admiral Blake Lawrence."

The band played "Hail to the Chief."

President Abigail Steele wore a red silk chiffon evening gown and matching red shoes from Narciso Rodriguez, the New Jersey-born Cuban-American designer. Knowing her skin was unquestionably her greatest accessory, she wore an understated single strand of pearls to present a bracingly clean, deceptively simple, elegantly modern woman.

Lawrence, taller than Abby by a half foot, wore the full dress naval regalia of a four-star admiral, including eight rows of combat medals and foreign decorations. He looked every inch the nation's dashing hero.

Blake's once-blond hair, now steel gray, was cut close in military fashion. Weathered skin from his many years on the oceans enhanced his seafaring appearance. Although not visible from a distance, age lines creased his cheeks and the corners of his eyes. The lines at the edges of his mouth deepened an already easy smile.

They strolled to the beat of a drum. He held his right arm in a half-bent manner, her gloved hand wrapped over the mass of gold braid that covered the sleeve of his blue uniform.

As they passed a Secret Service agent he heard the muffled, cryptic words of one agent speaking through a lip-mike to another, "POTUS (short for President of the United States) passing. Clear."

Without turning his head, he whispered, "You look beautiful."

"Thank you, sir," she responded with a slight tilt of her chin in his direction. Her large blue eyes continued to sweep the room, and she smiled to all.

They took their places at the head of the receiving line. Lawrence, more a student of the White House than President Steele, surveyed the room, modeled after the neoclassical English houses of the late 18th century. Below a ceiling with cornices of white plaster were natural oak wall paneling, Corinthian pilasters, and a delicately carved frieze. Famous paintings hung at eye level around the room. Against the walls were three antique console tables; a silver-plated chandelier and wall sconces added to the decor. Ornamental bronze-doré pieces served as table decorations. The 14-foot plateau centerpiece had seven mirrored sections fully extended. Standing bacchantes holding wreaths for tiny bowls and candles bordered the plateau. Three fruit baskets supported by female figures held flowers. Two rococo-revival candelabra dating from the Hayes administration were placed at each end of the formal dining table.

The furniture, objects, and paintings are the true residents of the White House, Blake thought. People are merely transients.

The dinner guests filed by, shaking hands with the president as the aide read their names and introduced them. She stood first in line; next came the admiral as her guest and consort. Then came Vice President Daniel Bowie Muñoz and his wife, the secretaries of State and Defense as well as two members of Congress with their spouses, all in proper order.

Admiral Lawrence led President Steele to her seat at the head of the mahogany dining table, surrounded by Queen Anne-style chairs, squeezing her hand as he guided her. Holding her chair as she slid into place, he whispered in her ear, "See you later?"

"I look forward to it," she whispered, still smiling to the guests who waited at their places designated by gold-embossed names on table cards.

The admiral walked to his place at the other end. She waited until he reached his chair, again smiled, and nodded for the others to take their seats.

Above the din of early conversation, Abby announced, "It was Andrew Jackson…" A hush came over the table. "…who first called this the 'State Dining Room'. You already knew that, didn't you? Of course. But, I just learned it before coming down." She laughed. "Shows you how much presidents know about this superb home. I also learned previous Presidents used it for formal dinners, although originally much smaller…" she pointed. "…and it served, at various times, as a drawing room, an office, and as a cabinet room. It now can seat as many as 140 guests. With that bit of history, a contrived opening on my part, I admit, I welcome you all to supper in the White House. I sincerely want you to enjoy yourselves. Chat with the other interesting people sitting near you. Everyone has a story. Toward the end of dinner, a wonderful Romanian string ensemble will play for us."

~ ~ ~ ~

After dinner Blake walked deliberately through the rear entrance. He returned the salute of the young Marine who knew in advance that the admiral would come into the private apartments of the president. The corporal's head remained fixed dead-ahead, but his eyes twinkled and momentarily darted after the lean form in a tan sports jacket and foulard ascot.

Lawrence returned the friendly nod of the Secret Service officer who stood in the passageway outside the president's second floor quarters.

"Evening, George," he said as he approached the door.

"Evening, admiral." Unlike the Marine's knowing, confidential look, George's remained impassive.

The newspapers reported many hypotheticals about their arrangement. Pundits drew conclusions about what happened after the hand-in-hand walks in the presidential gardens from photographs by the paparazzi. The tabloids asked, "Is the admiral President Steele's lover?"

He knocked and entered.

"That you, Blake?" came a voice from off the living room.

"Yes."

"Want a scotch?" she asked.

"Wouldn't mind. How about you, POTUS?"

"Not yet. I'm still changing out of this beautiful gown. Help yourself though. And I wish you'd quit calling me 'POTUS.'"

"What?" He'd lost some of his hearing, the result of too much gunfire and helicopter noise.

Her muffled voice rose an octave. "I said to help yourself. Wasn't that a nice dinner?"

Blake poured two fingers of Johnnie Walker Gold and took a seat on the couch while she changed. Whisper jumped to his lap. As he stroked her head, Blake took a sip of scotch. He held up the glass and looked at the presidential seal embossed on it.

She's come a long way, he mused.

Abigail Cass Steele, her auburn hair brushed back tightly and tied in Spanish elegance with a bun at the nape of her neck and dressed in gray tailored slacks and a red turtleneck sweater, walked into her living room.

Lawrence's eyes traveled first to her legs, then her hips, then focused on her breasts. His eyes then rose to her face. His mind drifted to their first meeting: He, a young midshipman, she, a student at Barnard. *She still has the same angelic look, except for those devilish ocean-blue eyes which can switch from hot to cool. She seems like two different people: Elegant and dignified in public, very feminine when we're alone.*

Her eyes caressed him. Leaning forward, her body language danced.

She doesn't need to entice me, she already owns me.

"I like the color red." His eyes focused again on her breasts, now propped up by an underwire bra. "If you looked any sexier you wouldn't need..."

"I know what you like. Not so fast." She touched her hair. "I *will* take that scotch now, just two fingers." She paused. "Hear the one about the crow sitting on a tree, doing nothing all day? A small rabbit saw the crow and asked him, 'Can I also sit like you and do nothing all day long?' The crow answered, 'Sure, why not?' So, the rabbit sat on the ground below the crow and rested. All of a sudden a fox appeared, jumped on the rabbit, and ate it. Management lesson: To sit and do nothing, you must sit very, very high up."

"Heard it," Blake said, deadpan. "Old joke."

"I like the punch line best. I *do* sit very high up."

He stared at her for a moment with no expression on his face, and then broke into laughter.

"You do like it," she beamed.

Her sincere, sometimes-naive eyes brought back memories of angels he saw at a church during his youth.

"Getoutahere. Of course I like it. Still a good one. You *are* going to be careful about telling those kinds of jokes outside this room, aren't you?"

"Oh, don't worry. Buck told me that one. Can't remember the circumstances. Probably on one of our trips to Pittsburgh. He tended to become more ornery in his hometown."

"I never knew Buck very well." He took a sip of scotch. "We only met twice, once in Pittsburgh and once in Saginaw at some event you had at CASS Corporation. I liked him. Mister Personality."

Abby's eyes closed for a moment as she remembered her husband, a ruggedly handsome business genius. She threw down a shot of Johnnie Walker's finest. "Ready for some pool?"

"Why not?" Blake followed her into what was once a drawing room with the original furniture now stored in a warehouse with the other historical White House items. The room appeared practically bare except for a top-of-the-line Brunswick billiard table sitting in the center of the room surrounded by a cue rack and trophy shelves. A wall held four feathered darts stuck in a circular board.

"Shoot you for the break?" she asked.

"I'm not giving it to you, if that's what you're asking."

Abby gently stroked the cue ball. It rolled slowly across the table until it came to rest near the rail.

Blake sent his ball just as softly, but his kissed the rail. "Damn it. Okay, lucky, your break."

"Watch your language, sailor. Hah, luck. No, pure skill. Rack 'em tight."

Lawrence drew the triangle from under the table, arranged the balls, and then spotted them. Almost simultaneous with his removal of the triangle, she slammed the cue ball. It smacked the one ball, and the rest spread across the green. One slid into a side pocket. The President stepped back and analyzed the table.

"Hmm, okay, angel face," he said, "this is like taking candy from a baby."

Her face reddened, eyes flashed. "Don't call me that," she snapped. "That's what Buck called me. I didn't like it then. Don't like it now."

"Sorry. It just came out. No POTUS. No angel face. Guess I can't call you any of my favorite names." He looked at her, puzzled.

"Oh, I'm sorry, too. I'm a bit edgy tonight. It's the China incident." She reached and touched his face. Then in a sensual gesture, she kissed him lightly on the lips. "I shouldn't have bit."

She stepped back again and looked at her options. When she bent to stroke the cue, her bracelet touched the green cloth.

His mouth twisted into a thin smile. "Your bracelet is going to drag and spoil your shot."

She stood. "You're trying to ice me, aren't you?" She lifted her head and winked at him. "Well, forget it. Six ball in the side pocket." She coolly sank five balls in a row before stopping again to analyze the table.

She's not tapioca, Blake thought.

Just as she prepared to fire again, Blake said, "What's this about the Chinese?"

She let it fly and missed the shot.

"Oops, I interrupted you. Want another try?"

"Nope. Your turn." Her jaw set.

"Go ahead and take that shot over," he teased. *She won't. She's the stuff mountains are made of; take your chances, never whine or snivel.*

"I said no." An edge entered her words.

Blake chalked his cue tip, scanned the table and took aim. "I repeat, as easy as..."

"You haven't shot yet. Don't get nervous. Oh, and about the Chinese," she said, "they shot down one of our planes. We don't know if our crew survived or why the Chinese pilots did it. Sam Talau, who I'm told you know intimately, reminded me about a Chinese plan to control the Indian Ocean."

Still lining up the shot, Blake spoke over his shoulder. "My roommate for four long years in

'Mother B,' Bancroft Hall on the Severn. If by 'intimate' you mean I saw him in his skivvies more than his mother and his wife put together... and anyway, I already knew about the attack from the evening papers. He stalled, stepped away from his shot and rested the cue on the floor.

"Well, Sam said if Russia cuts the Pan-Asian pipeline, China will not only fight back but likely put on a full-court press for oil from the Gulf and the South China Sea. We could be shut off. Bull Mullin wants me to declare war immediately and retaliate. Strike first. You agree?"

"Probably not. Bull has his failings. He's a good soldier, but he's also *very* political. By the way, your disagreement with the Bull made the papers — the *POST*. Someone let it leak."

"Tell me about his failings."

"You already know them."

"Hmm."

He recognized that sound when she muddled over a thought.

"Yes, I'm beginning to admit I do," she said. "And I wonder if I made a mistake making him chairman."

"Maybe it's because he has good hair — black, no gray, parted down the middle," Blake grinned. "Why *did* you pick him?"

Abby leaned against the pool table. "A compromise for the military-industrial boys. I knew Bull when I served in the Senate. Not well. I knew his name and listened on the few occasions when he made a report directly to Congress. He spent most of his time in the Pentagon and sent others to talk to us. I always thought it as the D.C. superior-inferior thing, like the 'I don't work for you' attitude which resides heavily in this town. One only talks to one's equal. Bull, a poster boy for behind-the-scenes and back-slapping, worked on senior senators, not juniors like me.

Blake stepped back from the table and leaned against a wall.

"I am fond of his wife," she mused aloud. "What's her name? Florence, yes, Florence. I remember her more than him. Very sweet. Maybe too sweet. But she is a trooper. A woman married to an Army man, for that matter any military wife, has to be a special person. I told my daughter Anna that when she decided to marry a West Pointer. I only knew Florence from a few social events and fundraisers. She always reminded me of Melanie from *Gone With the Wind,* tiny, fragile, and dainty, the delicate epitome of femininity, yet not weak or she couldn't make it to the top of the mountain with Bull. Maybe she thinks of him as her Rhett Butler. Probably thinks I'm the bottom of the sin basket, rock bottom. Anyway, Bull is my problem."

"You never asked me about Bull before you appointed him," Blake said.

"What would you have told me?"

"Today's military is very politicized and Bull's in the thick of it. In my time, three things were not discussed: Religion, politics, and women."

"How boring," she said.

"Today it's all out there, particularly politics. You know he's a closet redneck, a good ol' boy."

"Everyone knows it. At one time, a good ol' boy was simply a bigoted, uneducated white male. I remember at Barnard, we girls thought it just a Southern WASP phenomenon. Not so today." She shook her head as she rubbed blue chalk over the tip of her cue stick. "Of course nothing defies definition more than the term 'good ol' boy.' Certainly, one would not expect the chairman of the Joint Chiefs to be one."

"But he is and also a closet bigot."

"I'm sure he finds a lot wrong with me: A woman and president. Hmm. What do we have here? Is it because I'm a woman and have a man-friend, or does he have an eye on the White House?"

"Maybe all of the above. And to answer your earlier question, we don't need another resource war."

"Go ahead, shoot," she offered.

Blake put his cue back on the table and lined it up. He sank several balls before he missed.

Abby took over and cleaned the table. "Rack 'em." She watched while he gathered the balls. "What do you know about this resource war issue?"

"We've had it on our radar for years. It's been a long time coming. It's what the Gulf War was all about." Blake shifted backward, expecting the cue ball to slam, but Abby held off. "I'm not an expert on the global resource problem as a whole, but it could become a whole new ball game. You better ask Sam to bring in his CIA experts. He has a guy named Plato, Dr. Plato Perestrello Wang, a strange name for a Chinese-American. Smart as hell."

"Good idea, but I'm a step ahead. He's already coming over tomorrow morning. Want to sit in?"

"Can't. Already scheduled. Oh, and remind me sometime to brief you on the Chinese strategy called Assassin's Mace."

She nodded then stroked the cue ball into the pack and watched two of them fall. After easily running a series, she came to a position that required a bridge. She hiked her leg like a man over the edge of the table and slid the long stick across the felt surface, resting it on the bridge near the cue ball.

Sometimes I think she's more man than woman. The world better watch out if she uses her "take no prisoners" approach to life in the global arena.

After a few more games they adjourned to the living room where they sipped a glass of wine. Blake looked at her more closely, savoring the air of grace. He reached across, stroked her hand (their prelude to romance) and asked, "You want to dance? I'll start the music?"

The corners of her mouth turned upward.

He switched on the stereo and took her in his arms. They swayed to the tune. He touched her hair and bent to kiss her, his hand moving down her back. She returned the kiss but then pulled away. He sensed her mood change.

"Not tonight, darling," she said. "Would you mind if I closed out early? I've got China on my mind, as if I didn't have anything else to worry about."

"It's always your call, POTUS, I mean Abby. I can see my way out. One of these days you'll have to marry me so we can put an end to this foolishness."

She smiled. "You know… Maybe… Time's just not right."

He put his arm around her shoulders in a hug. His lips touched her forehead and again on her mouth. He knew how she felt about losing her husband, so he didn't push the proposal. He opened the door to leave.

"Would you mind if I sent you on a special mission?" she asked.

He stopped and leaned against the frame. "Of course not. Like what?"

"Like going to China. I don't trust Bull and I'm unsure of Alseño."

"You appointed Alseño."

"Yes, both of them… and that also may have been a mistake. Alseño may be too close to the military-industrial complex."

"He brought you a lot of campaign money."

"I get campaign money from many sources. My problem is we're not getting intel through State or CIA. I have to find out what's really happening. Oh, and can I recall you to active duty?"

"Roosevelt called up MacArthur twice. You *are* president of *the* United States. You can do practically anything you want."

"Not everything, darling."

"Are you sure you don't want to dance?"

"Maybe when you get back from China."

~ **Five** ~

Abigail Steele awoke at exactly five every morning without an alarm. Instead of putting her feet on the floor and getting to her work, she lingered. Blake had set off for China on an early morning presidential plane, and her first thoughts fixed on him and his proposal of marriage. *I do care for him. Should I or shouldn't I?*

She broke from her languid moment, jumped out of bed, and took a quick shower.

Over breakfast she reviewed the first editions of several papers and listened to the early TV news shows. She watched her press secretary Midget Berry explained how Chinese fighters shot down the surveillance plane.

"No word yet about the crew," Berry added, then cleverly ducked both of the snidely worded questions from an opposition-leaning reporter who implied Abby slept with a lover in the White House and about a division between the president and her Joint Chiefs chairman.

Good for you, Midget.

Ready for her day, Abby strode toward a briefing about China and resource wars.

Betty Porter ushered Sam Talau, the CIA's expert, and Secretary of State Wilmer Flanagan into the Oval Office.

Abby first greeted Wilmer. The gaunt, slender, white-haired elder statesman of her cabinet touched his tie knot to check his immaculate attire. "Abby, it's always good to see you."

She drew him aside. "Anything heard from the Chinese?"

"Not a word, ma'am." Wilmer said in a subdued voice.

"I sent Lawrence."

"He called me before he left this morning."

"Thank you Wilmer." She turned and smiled. "Your turn, Napoleon."

"Madam President," Sam nodded, "May I introduce Doctor Plato Perestrello Wang."

The men looked like fireplugs. Sam, a short bullet of energy ready to explode, the hardened athlete, stood next to the slightly shorter, timid-appearing, roly-poly, awkward professor.

"How do you do, Doctor Wang."

Plato responded with the twinkle of a prankster and a wide smile across a full face that emphasized his oriental eyes. "How do you do, madame, as the French would address you." He gave a short bow.

"I'm curious. Tell me about the name 'Perestrello.' It's not French, is it?" Abby asked.

"Well, no. My mother is Chinese and my father Portuguese; thus the curious name. He always claimed to be a direct descendent of Christopher Columbus on his mother's side. I also use my Chinese name, which is Wang. I grew up in China. I know the culture as well as the Punonghua, or Mandarin language, and all the dialects of that country: Cantonese, Shanghaiese, Fukienese or Hahka, plus several variations of each."

"You also speak French?"

"French? Yes, I learned it during my academic travels."

"He failed to tell you he enters and leaves China easily and often," Sam inserted. "No one asks how. Also, Madam President, his Ph.D. is from Harvard, where he teaches Chinese history and culture from time to time."

"Hmm. Impressive. Proceed, Dr. Perestrello, or should I call you Dr. Wang?"

"Plato will do, madame." He bowed slightly. "I'm much honored to have this opportunity to meet you and conduct this briefing, Madame President."

His British English mixed with a slight Asian patois showed the richness of his education.

"This should take less than thirty minutes, madame. I'm told you were briefed on much of the material."

Plato paused while Abby took a seat.

He opened as if giving a lecture. "One of the things we know about earth is that between 1970 and the present, human activity has depleted one-third of earth's natural wealth: Fresh cover, fresh water, marine fisheries, and fossil fuel.

"We also know between 1950 and the present, Gross World Product increased 583 percent, from 6 trillion to 41 trillion in constant dollars. Global per capita income grew from about $2,500 to $6,750. The world is on a wealth roll, though somewhat unevenly.

"As the pace of industrialization has exploded, so has our energy consumption. The human community expands by 80 million people a year, and the need for petroleum and other energy sources has never been greater, which also has a major influence on global warming."

President Steele squinted as she read the numbers arrayed bullet-style on his chart. She made a few notes. She sopped up numbers like eating a good onion soup; consequently she often got ahead of her briefer.

"This planet has some *big* problems," she said.

"Indeed it does, Madame President. World population is about 8 billion. India's population will soon exceed China's, which is already a billion and a half. In the United States alone, the number of car miles rose from 1.5 trillion in 1982 to over 4 trillion today. Of the natural resources in short supply, oil is the highest concern. Oil is the center of your security policy. We must have access to and protect vital global resource flows."

"I wasn't the first to see that," Abby said. "Alfred Mahan, a Navy captain, first articulated the warning. Teddy and Franklin Roosevelt, Jimmy Carter, Bill

Clinton, both Bushes had the same policy." She motioned Plato to continue.

"China's energy consumption between the year 2000 and now has grown at about five percent, four times that of the USA and the European Union combined. As of 1986, China, no longer self-sufficient, had become a major oil importer. They have invested heavily in overseas oil fields as well as the Pan-Asian continental oil-bridge, an oil and gas pipe that links China with the Caspian Sea region in central Asia."

She listened only partially. Her thoughts drifted to the problems her predecessors left her. *Resource shortages, global warming, a shaky economy, and now China.*

Plato pointed to a line on the map. "You see, China no longer wants to be dependent on *yang you* sold to them by *yang quizi.*"

She came alert. *"Yang you, yang quizi?"*

"Yang you means 'foreign oil,' and *yang quizi* means 'foreign devils'." He paused. "No questions? ...I continue. Much of China's history has been dominated by the problem of providing enough food for its people. America has about 300 million. China passed that threshold ages ago, but by the miracle process of early ripening of rice with two and sometimes three crops a year, they solved their food problem.

"Today they pursue a different problem — oil. In their technology-based economy, people have cars and use fossil fuel at enormous rates. The Persian Gulf is still the epicenter of known, proven oil reserves. Yes, there are reserves in Siberia, Argentina, the North Atlantic, and even the South China Sea, but nothing compared to the Middle East. Everything is okay so long as there is stability in that region, so when oil was discovered in the Caspian Sea, China jumped on it. So did America," he emphasized. "If you recall, we even deployed troops in a big war exercise in 1997, and of course, our manhunt back in '01 and '02 for Osama bin Laden and al-Qaeda in Afghanistan put us right in the mix."

"This is one of the things the entire world could end up fighting over." Abby said. "There must be an alternative to fossil fuel that would resolve their shortage."

"Madame," he said soberly. "In the short term, oil *is* the only answer."

~ Six ~

Marine Captain Walter "Razor" Billings, call sign Box One, the leader of a combat air patrol and his wingman, First Lieutenant C.J. "Pipes" Walston, call sign Box Two, orbited their amphibious formation. Strapped in their cockpits tighter than a moth's cocoon, surrounded by a wall of flight instruments, a built-in weapons console and a heads up display (HUD) projected on the cockpit windshield; Razor figured they looked like Neil Armstrong going to the moon.

"Box One, take bogies, closing this position from the south," came from the Airborne Early Warning Aircraft (AWAC) Controller. His voice sounded a bit tweaked. "This is a no-shitter. Hostile. Weapons free. Our electronics shows two JH-10A Chinese strike fighters. Maybe the same ones that shot down our MMA near the Spratlys."

"Roger, Box One, taking." Razor grunted to his wing, "Push it up, Pipes. Burner. Now. Tapes on."

"Roger, burner, tapes."

Razor's thoughts jumped. *Mission: Protect the ships below from air attack. Rules of engagement: Simple, weapons free. Yeah, that means no bullshit negotiations, no gray shit. We can shoot — simple, easy to remember.*

From cruise at 28,000 feet and .85 mach, he watched as the needle jumped. When he reached supersonic speed, Razor checked his fuel and thought. *We'll need a tank on the way home.* His hand lightly touched the punch-out lever, just in case. *Hot shit, now we'll find out if these new strike fighter vertical take-off birds are better than the JH-10. Not since the Korean War have we gone head-to-head with the PRC.*

Razor held only one on his radar, so he rolled into a right turn and headed south. He glanced over his shoulder and saw Pipes stick with him like super glue.

"Box One, lead," Razor said to confirm he had the lead Chinese aircraft. He knew Pipes would auto on the follower.

"Craniums up, Pipes." His voice jumped about two octaves. "Shit's gonna happen."

Razor checked for a friendly squawk. "Nobody home."

"Roger. ID," Pipes said.

With the targets thirty nautical miles out, he said to himself, *"Better stoke it up."*

"Box Two, full burner," Razor ordered.

"Roger, gate, max," Pipes spit out the fighter talk with a professional tone.

"Box Two, arm hot."

Pipes' fuel tanks came off. Bright flames shot out from under the wing.

"Roger, Box Two armed."

When well over mach, he punched off his own tanks, and the jet jumped abruptly. He looked back and saw his stabilizers still intact. *Good.*

"I see break out. Two, spread. No, stacked," Razor corrected himself. "Lead."

The contacts separated into two well-defined pieces of electronics.

"Roger, trail," Pipes confirmed.

"Box One spiked. Twenty degrees left." Razor had a warning his aircraft was illuminated by a threat radar.

"Box Two, same," Pipes responded.

"Crank right and split." Razor conducted a defensive right-turn maneuver. He saw Pipes juke also and move away.

As soon as he shook the Chinese illumination, he focused on the intercept. His eyes fixed on the HUD. *See the whole field, baby.*

Razor switched his miniraster on the leader, a concentration of electronic energy. As soon as his radar locked on, he thumbed forward to track-while-scanning so he could search airspace and be locked on at the same time.

He now held the lead aircraft seventeen degrees left, and his first shot would come off inside sixteen nautical miles. He squeezed the pickle. The missile seemed to take an eternity before it actually launched. "Come on, damn it. Go baby." He heard the loud whoosh above the wind, even with radio comms, earplugs, and a helmet in the cockpit and felt the rocket motor jump off the rails. *Wow.* He watched the flames shoot out from the tail end of the missile and the smoke and contrails follow it.

"FOX 3, 18K," he called.

"Roger, ditto," Pipes barked, confirming the range to target.

Razor's heart rate spun out of control. It felt like he reached his aerobic limit. Against broken clouds he saw a thin dot.

"Tally ho, nose seven miles, climbing." He had visual on the lead and hoped Pipes would follow up with a tally call on the trailer. Approaching five miles, he scanned behind the leader for the trailer. *No joy. Shit, did Pipes get off?*

He stepped to lock up the trailer. Inside five nautical miles Razor thumbed to another missile. He tried to uncage, but the tone wasn't there. He again pressed and held the pickle.

"Come on, damn it. Launch, baby," he yelled.

Both targets did a check turn to the southwest and descended to the low teens.

They're trying to avoid our missiles.

The two Marines closed for another shot when, between the HUD and the canopy bow at 12:30 position, Razor saw the leader explode like torches at a Hawaiian luau party, swinging through the air with flames from the tail.

Seconds later the trailer exploded into a streaking blaze from the tail even as Razor tried to uncage another missile. *Never mind. Shit, I should have trusted Pipes.*

"Splash two," Razor shrilled. His eyes followed the fireballs; then he saw the chutes that confirmed both pilots ejected safely. "Not that we would give a shit if they morted."

"Roger, splash two," the controller acknowledged. "Thanks. Good shooting."

"Box One, naked."

"Box Two, naked."

"Pipes, go buster."

"Roger, pure," Pipes said.

Razor made a hard turn to the north and headed for the tanker. He let Pipes take the boom first, and then he slid in for a drink. As soon as he refueled he joined on Pipes. "Out of here, baby."

"That was top of the hog." Razor bellowed.

"You got that right." Pipes quipped.

They rolled in and settled their vertical take-off and landing (V/STOL) planes to a hover side by side. On deck, after they pulled into de-arm, Razor saw a freak in a flight suit and reflective belt jumping up and down. *Wow, the skipper welcomed us back. He must have gotten the word from the controller.* Everyone came running out like a bunch of kids waiting for the ice cream truck. Before popping the canopy, Razor called out on the ops freq, "Pipes, you're a sweet shit."

"Yeah, tell it to the boys."

They climbed out, and the skipper shook his hand first, followed by the mob. They all laughed, shouted, and hooted along with high-fives and hugs.

"Awesome." Razor let out a belly laugh.

He finally broke through the crowd to find Pipes. He opened his arms wide to wrap around his wingman. Her helmet came off, she unpinned her hair, and blond curls fell on sweaty shoulders. She smiled, showing those radiant pearls he could never forget.

~ **Seven** ~

A midday beam of golden light spread across the Oval Office. Glancing through the windows, Abby saw meandering pathways lined with hedges and flowers. Beyond, tourists walked and talked, carefree in their curiosity. She sat amidst a flock of people vying for her attention. *How did four people get into my office all at once?* She checked her watch. *Tough, I'm leaving.*

"Time out, ladies and gentlemen. Its lunch hour, and I have an important engagement." She hurried toward the door.

Betty Porter snapped to attention, her hands extended along the seams of her Navy blue slacks.

"Er, Madam President, this is most important and..." Wilmer Flanagan protested while the rest looked bewildered.

"Wilmer," she interrupted, "everything's important. It's China this and European Union that." She held up papers. "Some things are more so." She exited the room and walked toward her quarters. "Betty, have the car brought around."

"Aye aye, ma'am." Her voice tensed, "Going somewhere, Madam President? It's not on the schedule."

"Just do it, please."

"Aye, aye, ma'am. Do you want me to come along?"

"Not this time, Betty."

Abby's secretary, Margarite Wellaby, small in stature with heavy glasses, large nostrils and skin as pale as paper, grabbed the remaining papers from the President's desk. She ran after President Steele. "Shall I hold these for your signature when you return or..."

Abby raised her hands to the sky. "Oh, Margarite, all right, I'll take them with me and sign them while they bring the cars. Meet me at the portal, dear." She left Margarite standing outside the office, hurried down the corridor, and entered her private quarters.

Anna Steele Perks put down her teacup and stood up. "Betty made me feel at home, Mom."

"Darling." Abby gave her a hug and kiss. "Been waiting long? My word, you look more like Grandmother Lucile everyday: The red hair — her figure too, she had a body, didn't she? How are my grandchildren? Is Third doing well at Barnard?"

"Not really and yes, the kids are fine, Mom."

"Where do you want to eat?" Abby absently glanced at the several official papers, placed them on the table and scribbled her signature.

"I thought we would eat here."

"No, let's go out. The day is so beautiful." she said without looking up.

"Go out? Can you do that?"

"Yes. You've already eaten here at the White House and I need to get out of this place. Let's go to the Pickle Factory. How did you get here?"

"Secret Service drove me. The Pickle Factory? That's not the best place in town."

"I have the car waiting. When your father and I were in town, we used to eat there with real people. Come along."

Abby marched to the driveway where three Secret Service agents, her driver, and her secretary waited. "Margarite, darling, please give this to Secretary Flanagan. Tell him I'll sign the rest when I return."

"Good afternoon, Madam President," the senior Secret Service officer said. Handsome and athletic-looking, his black suit showed a bulge under the left arm. A thin microphone at his lips connected to tiny receiver plugged into his right ear. "You know the dangers of going into the community."

"George, this is random enough. I'm going to the Pickle Factory. Anna and I will be there for about forty-five minutes. I hate feeling like a prisoner. You know the place?"

"Yes, ma'am. However, we'll drive slowly. We need a bit of time to position our team. The D.C. police have a right to a heads-up."

"Okay," she said. "Round 'em up."

He spoke into his microphone, "Heads up. POTUS on the move."

45

The limousine slowly pulled out of the driveway and onto Pennsylvania Avenue. Inside, Abby took her daughter's hand. "Everything going okay?"

"Except Murph's sweating the promotion to general and the kids being teenagers, everything is swell." The sarcasm spilled like water over Niagara. "Does being a mother ever get easy? The twins start college next year, and Third's doing well, I think. She's supposed to graduate in June."

"Wonderful, and the third generation to graduate from Barnard," Abby laughed. "And don't worry about his promotion."

"The way you said that thounds like you would interfere. He doesn't want that," Anna said, her lisp more pronounced when uncomfortable.

"I just meant not to worry, dear." Abby squeezed Anna's hand. "Murphy will do well." She changed the subject. "Anna, what do you hear from Richard? He's been quiet lately. I'm not sure he ever approved of my becoming president."

"Oh, we talked for a few minutes last week. He's very busy. He said to tell you that he'll call soon. He hates the Secret Service hanging around his building."

Richard Steele, her physician son, lived and practiced in Pittsburgh, where he studied medicine at Pitt more than twenty years before. He stayed on as a researcher, focusing on the elderly, a carry-over interest from time spent caring for his paternal grandparents during his college days.

"He never returns my calls. He once sent a message through a Secret Service agent I should stop calling and if he wanted to talk, he would call. When you talked to him, did he sound all right?" Abby asked.

"Sound all right? You mean did he sound manic or depressed?"

"Yes. Did his voice sound normal? He talks to you. Your father and I could tell when he was on a high or low and irritated or had a problem. He's always been a bit reclusive."

"Oh, he's still a prig, but he sounded okay to me. Must be on his meds."

"I do worry about him, always will. Bipolar is such an insidious disorder." Abby looked at her hands then out the window. "Look, dear. Real street-Americans just walking around, some even in shirt-sleeves. What a beautiful day. One of those strange Washington days that feels like July." She looked back at Anna. "Sorry. You were saying?"

"I'm finished."

The line of cars stopped in front of the building where an unpretentious sign read "Pickle Factory." People streamed in and out of one of the most popular eateries in Washington. At the sight, Abby felt warm and wanted to move among them.

Before the car door opened, agents jumped out and ran to get into position. As Abby and Anna strolled toward the steps leading to the second floor, many well-wishers waved and sang out, "Good afternoon and hi, Madam President." One woman in a naval uniform saluted. Yet the agents directed the pedestrians to stay away.

Abby disregarded the agents' protectiveness, which she considered overdone, and shook hands with everyone she passed. She stopped to chat with a mother dressed in running togs with a baby strapped to her chest.

Once inside the restaurant, the waiter ushered them to a table with a view of the Potomac River. Abby sniffed. "Smells exactly as I remember. Briny pickles, hot dogs, burgers cooking on grills, and me among ordinary Americans."

A college-aged waiter wearing a black bow tie with the sleeves of his white shirt rolled up approached their table. "Order, ma'am?" he asked without intimidation by POTUS.

"I'll have a glass of Coors Lite. Reminds me of Ronald Reagan and the Pittsburgh Steelers. They were big fans of the beer when it first became popular. Anna, how about you?"

"No. Unlike you, I have to watch my waistline. Just water for me, thank you."

"I'll be back in a minute to take your food order, Madam President," the young man said. "Oh, and the boss said to tell you the meal and drinks are on the house."

"Where *is* the boss?"

"Oh, he'll be here soon, ma'am. No one told him you were coming. He said you'd understand."

"Not to worry, I know how that is."

The women continued their conversation about Anna's children when a short man with dark hair and deep-set eyes rushed toward the table. Abby jumped up. Waving off two Secret Service men with guns drawn, she gave him a big hug. "Henry."

"Madam President, Madam President, I'm a so sorry. Is everything all right? Why don't you call? I make something special." His voice still carried the accent he brought from Italy.

"Everything's fine. Just lovely, Henry. Good to see you again," she turned. "Anna, this is Henry Pasquinelli, an old friend. He grew up in your dad's neighborhood back in Pittsburgh. I've been coming here for years, isn't that right, Henry?"

"Of course, Madam President. However, we haven't seen you recently. How long has it been?"

"More than a year. Although I had good intentions to come, circumstances have changed from my days as a regular. How is Doris?"

"She's good. When I told her you come, she say to tell you hello but she keep talking. You know how she talk, atalk, atalk." Henry spoke to the waiter who arrived with the drinks. "Take a good care of the president."

"Yes, sir." The young man straightened and grinned.

"Oh, and Henry, thanks for offering on-the-house food, but I can't accept. That agent will pay the bill." She pointed to George standing against the wall with another man, both in dark suits.

After Henry left, Abby and Anna ordered the house special, a "San Francisco Dog," mostly salad surrounding a wiener on a bun, accompanied by big slices of dill pickles.

"Now," Abby announced, "let's get down to business. It sounds like your crew is just about out of the nest. When can you come to work?"

"Mom, we've talked about this before, but I did discuss it with Murphy. He's uncomfortable with the thought of his wife working in the White House while he's in the Pentagon."

"Oh, pooh. It's been done before. I need you close to me. There are things... Look, may I talk to Murphy? We get along very well. I even think he likes me. Who ever heard of a husband liking a mother-in-law, especially one like me? I'll have a desk put in and ready for you next week. Just a few hours a day, that's all.

"A few hours a day? That's a laugh. Neither you nor Dad could work just a few hours, like when you ran CASS Corporation, you gave twenty. And now you're president... Hah, I know you, Mother."

"Do you mind?"

"Mind what?"

"My talking to Murphy."

"Oh, I guess not. But I'll do it only if he approves and I can get the twins organized. Tell me again why you need me nearby. Why can't we just talk on the telephone?"

"Darling, this town is full of wags with egos bigger than the heavens and ambitions overflowing like a river in a rainstorm. People get their priorities mixed up all the time. I have no spouse. Your father would have been the kind of confidant I need, but he's gone. Not that he would have been happy as the first gentleman. You do know I have a relationship with Admiral Lawrence, don't you?"

"Oh, him." Anna's lips pursed and shook her head slowly.

"You don't approve. It's mostly friendship."

"Mostly friendship? That's a stretch. That's not what the whithpering public thinks."

"He's more than a friend. I've known him a long time, since Barnard. Before your father in fact."

"Sleeping over is serious, Mom."

"God, I'm a grandmother. I can have a man friend."

"But, it's like you're flaunting him, Mom. Everyone knows."

"I'm not flaunting him, but I'm not hiding him, either. Well, I need someone close to me who will tell it like it is. Who's plugged in and has a feel for the people. Your job would be to watch my six o'clock.

51

Keep your mother out of trouble and connected to our family."

"You have a whole staff to do that."

"Not the same. They look after my public image. I need someone to look after my private side."

"But what specifically will I do?"

"Don't know. Just be there."

"I'm not a world expert. I'm not an expert at anything. All I have are degrees from Barnard and Columbia law and a house full of Army brats. I'm working on a degree in raising kids."

Abby smiled at her daughter's assurance. "You know enough. You also mix with street Americans every day, shopping and such. Just be there. Keep me tuned in to real life. If nothing else then for moral support. You worked before you met Murphy. You and he know the Army," she whispered, "I may have a small Army problem. General Bull Mullin and I may not be made for each other. I think he's on a different frequency. He's pushing me toward war with China. He and the previous party represent the glorification of war, and you know how I hate that. Now, don't breathe a word of what I just said."

Anna reached across and touched her mother's arm. "Oh, Mom, of course not, never. As Dad used to say, 'Loose lips sink ships.'" Her voice dropped to a whisper. "Rumor has it in the Pentagon, according to Murphy, Bull plans to run for president."

President Steele's head bobbed. Although surprised by the news, she didn't comment.

As they rose to leave the Pickle Factory, she waved to everyone. The caravan of cars waiting in front had multiplied, causing a commotion not seen by most lunchtime crowds. Local police joined the Secret Service and had the place surrounded as if to catch a criminal.

George's phone rang. "Yes, yes. I will."

He turned to the president. "Madam President. You're wanted immediately in the Situation Room."

She waved goodbye to Henry and he ran to thank her. "You come back soon, Madam President, OK?"

"OK, Henry, I'll try."

"Gotta move out, ma'am. Can't linger," George urged.

Abby shook the police captain's hand and thanked him. "Would you see that my daughter gets home?"

She waited until Anna drove away. "Now we better roll, George."

She felt a pang of regret. Though she preferred to spend the rest of the day with Anna, she climbed into the rear seat of the limousine, her mind immediately switched to the next event. *Probably more problems with China.*

~ **Eight** ~

Abby arrived in the Situation Room to a flurry of activity and disorder. Midget had a confused look on her typically emotionless face. Her hands flew into the air. "Where is my assistant?"

Walter Coons, Abby's Chief of Staff, a bespectacled, chubby former governor of Michigan, wrangled with some underlings.

"What's going on, Walter?"

"I'm sorry, Madam President. Several important people are late. This never happens. We didn't expect you so soon. The Chinese ambassador is here to see you, early. He wasn't scheduled until three o'clock."

Secretary Flanagan, his arm full of papers and a briefing book, entered in a flurry. "I'm sorry, Madam President. I was in a meeting. I brought historical references."

Abby took her seat, even as others raced into the room.

"What is the emergency?" she asked.

"Our fighters shot down two Chinese J-10's," answered Reed Alseño.

"Who shot them down?"

"Two of our Marine fighters, ma'am."

"Where?" She asked calmly.

"Near the Spratlys again."

"We're the most powerful nation on earth, and we can't control our own forces?" she growled, her voice betraying a poisonous mood brought about by being called back from her lunch with Anna, the staff not ready for her arrival, and the Chinese ambassador waiting in the next room

"I said no retaliation until we knew more. My God! What happened to the little wars? Bosnia? Serbia? Kosovo? Afghanistan? Iraq? No wonder everyone hates us. How in the hell can we keep the peace when a couple of Marine fighter jocks shoot down two Chinese fighters? Who authorized it?"

Silence.

She waited for someone to speak. Looking quizzically first at the older Wilmer Flanagan then youthful Reed Alseño, she raised her hands, palms up.

Both men shook their heads and clearly knew nothing of the turn of events.

Bull Mullin walked in late but in time to hear the question and stood to one side of State and Defense. "No one has to authorize it," Bull smirked. His body language and tilt of his head showed his disdain.

Am I exaggerating this? Why is he so popular and I'm put off by him? Maybe it's the good ol' boy image with his southern patois. Look at his uniforms, uncaring and on the edge of sloppiness. They fit him like a private nearing the end of his enlistment.

"Tell her." He glared at the civilians. "Everyone knows those pilots have the right to defend themselves."

"No need to raise your voice," Abby bristled.

"Hell, this is war!" Bull responded. "Someone *should* raise *their voice*! We should strike the Chinese with surprise! They only know strength, not weakness. We can't procrastinate on this one." Bull nodded to Admiral Plexico Crocket, the Chief of Naval Operations, to indicate his turn to say something.

Crocket cleared his throat, "Ah-mm, well, ma'am, it seems a couple of Chinese JH-10A fighters, probably the same ones that hit our MMA, turned and advanced full heartedly toward one of our airborne early warning aircraft. The AWACS gave a 'weapons free' to their Marine fighter cover, and the Marines did both the Chinese fighters."

"*Did* them?"

"Sorry, ma'am," his face reddened, "shot them down."

"Are the Chinese pilots okay?"

"Yes, ma'am. Picked up by one of our ships from their life rafts. One had a broken arm. Hit the canopy on the way out of the plane."

"Any news yet on our crew?"

"No, ma'am. Still searching."

"Madam President, the Chinese ambassador waits in the Blue Room for you at this moment," Secretary Wilmer Flanagan interjected.

"Walter already told me, Wilmer."

Abby brought her right hand to her chin as if in deep thought. She raised her head. "Did someone say one of them was a woman?"

"One of who, ma'am?" Bull Mullin asked quizzically in his heavy accent from Macon, Georgia. His teeth showed tobacco stains, and he brought with him a smell of either smoking or chewing.

She wanted to say, "Whom, not who" but decided against it. "What are we talking about?" Her voice hardened, "Our fighter pilots? True?"

"Oh, yes, ma'am." Dan Bowie Muñoz, her usually docile vice president, sensed the friction. He quickly read from a briefing paper. "The wingman's name is Lieutenant Claudia J. 'Pipes' Walston."

Abby turned to Admiral Crocket. "And you say the Chinese pilots made a threatening move toward our forces?"

"Yes, ma'am."

"And our pilots beat them to the punch?"

"Yes, ma'am."

She rose to leave. "She must be damn good, true?"

Admiral Crocket's eyes brightened, a smile broke across his face and his color returned to its normal light tan color. "Damn good, ma'am. The J-10 is the best Chinese plane."

"Well," she said with a smile. "I'll see the Chinese ambassador now."

~ **Nine** ~

While her staff escorted Chinese ambassador Liu Chen Zhang Li to her, Abby reviewed a background that included a B.S. and M.S. from Beijing University and a Ph.D. from Harvard.

He wore the formal suit of stripes and tails with top hat and presented himself before her with a deep bow. Both hands extended, he presented her a nicely-wrapped gift. "From the Chinese premier, President Steele."

"Oh, no. I cannot accept this," she said, aware that in Asian cultures it's impolite to accept his first offer of a gift and to decline at least twice.

"The premier sends it with his personal regards." His arms were still extended.

"No, it is too much," her tone less certain.

"Please accept this as a present from the Chinese people."

"Thank you, Mr. Ambassador." She took the gift in her hands and nodded. "Please convey the sincere appreciation of the American people to your premier." She handed the gift to Betty Porter then picked up her gift to the Chinese people, a handmade piece of art made by a Native American from a Florida Everglades tribe. After describing its origin, she passed it to him, and then motioned for him to sit.

He did so after thanking her several times and giving the gift to his aide.

They each wished the other's families well and inquired about their health. He sat at rigid diplomatic attention. He punctuated his remarks with short bows of the head and an occasional dip at the waist.

In his black and white suit, he reminds me of a penguin, Abby thought.

With the diplomatic dance complete, Abby leaned forward and broached the topic of her agenda. "Ambassador, I need some answers. We know you are in a border dispute that could result in a war with Russia and could close your Pan-Asian pipeline. We know your country faces serious shortages of fossil fuel, and we share your concern for your people. But we also know your country has moved naval forces into the South China Sea near the Spratly Islands. Your fighters shot down one of our airplanes. Can you explain, please?"

Li's smile disappeared. "There is no proof it was our planes. Your planes shot down two of our fighters for no reason."

"Stop this nonsense, sir" Abby sparked. "Our plane reported two JH-10A Chinese fighters. It's a shame about your jets, but it would appear your pilots survived while ours may not since we still have a search out for them. All of this troubles me," Abby leaned forward, "Because we also have learned you recently enlarged your force in the area to a significant armada. I am told that China may take possession of the Spratlys. Is that true? To us, all of this seems dangerous, but at this stage it is only kindling. We do not wish it to become an inferno. We are a peaceful nation. I need to know, sir. What are China's intentions?"

Ambassador Li never blinked. "We have only peaceful intentions, but of course oil is of vital importance to our nation."

"Of course." Abby leaned back. "But remember, oil is important to many nations, not just China. It's a global problem. We are a nation of laws. We expect others to also respect the law. Please convey to your nation that it should not misstep on this matter, sir. It could lead to consequences no one wants. I strongly suggest you recall your naval force in the South China Sea and negotiate the Spratly matter and the border dispute at a high international level, maybe by the United Nations."

"If not?" he asked, never changing expression.

"If not, sir, I warn you: China or any other nation cannot disrupt the sea lanes. Violation of freedom of the seas is tantamount to a declaration of war."

~ Ten ~

As the chess game for the South China Sea played out, Wen Chen, China's vice-premier, stood on a remote mountaintop bordering southern Russia. He had been sent by President Sun Yuxi on a look-and-learn trip to this corner of land between Kazakhstan and Mongolia where thirty divisions of two of the world's most powerful nations faced off.

Slightly built with a military haircut, he wore a chemically gray Mao jacket that fit his bureaucratic image.

Before him stood rocket launchers, long-range artillery, and soldiers ready to fight. One word from Premier Sun Yuxi, and the war with Russia would begin.

Wen Chen, a trained geologist, asked the colonel who was escorting him, "Where is the pipeline?"

"Up there, sir." He pointed toward the Russian troop lines. "This side of our border. It's marked by barbed wire, sir. There," he pointed. "Where you see the flag markers."

"And theirs?"

"Well, they claim a line 20 kilometers into our territory, this side of the pipeline, near the border of that hamlet." He pointed behind them to a small village nestled in a valley between two mountains.

Before leaving Beijing, Chen had been briefed on the plan to ensure an adequate flow of fossil fuel into his country. The Chinese Pan-Asian continental oil-bridge stretched from Kazakhstan, on the Caspian Sea, across Uzbekistan and Tajikistan into the northern tip of China. The problem, he was told, was that Russia claims that spit of land. If the pipeline is cut, China will be forced to go to war with Russia and execute a broader plan that he knew was more about world status than oil security. He knew there were some in the government who envisioned hegemony, a new world order where China was the central player. If they had their way, taking the Spratly Islands would just be the beginning.

~ **Eleven** ~

Followed by her press secretary, President Steele left the Oval Office with long, purposeful strides. Her route took her past the executive staff offices, the Cabinet Room, and the Roosevelt Room. Midget raced to keep up.

Abby walked briskly to the lectern and nodded to the audience of reporters sitting in rows of chairs in the James S. Brady press room.

The voice of a prominent talking head, noted for his go-for-the-jugular style, shouted, "Madam President, what about your affair with Admiral Lawrence?"

Abby's cheeks flared to match the color of her hair. She leaned across the lectern and raised her head so the dimple in her chin pointed directly at him. She looked down her nose and stared at the man. The room silenced. She continued to stare until he blinked and glanced away. "Ladies and gentlemen," she announced, then softened her voice to command attention. "I will take questions later."

Abby opened her folder and scanned the notes placed there by staff. She looked up.

"Recently we've learned that the Chinese have deployed their naval forces into the South China Sea and that our airplanes encountered theirs. I am happy to announce the crew of our surveillance aircraft has survived." She paused. "I have expressed my concern directly to the Chinese ambassador. Our ambassador to China, Mr. Martin Chee, has conveyed our message of alarm to the leaders of that country.

"I sent Admiral Blake Lawrence as my special emissary to China to look into this dispute that threatens global peace. It is of particular interest to us because of the oil implications. We will continue to monitor the situation because of the potential problem in a world that already has more than enough strife. Next, I want to assure all Americans a full range of domestic issues are under study."

She finished by outlining the specifics of each of the important programs. "I'll now take a few questions."

The noise in the room burst like a birthday balloon. From everywhere came shouts for recognition, but above the din the same front-row reporter called, "Madam President, what about your affair with Admiral Lawrence?"

"Is it true that your son is manic-depressive?" another shouted.

The bastards, Abby thought. *They don't want to know about the tax implications of reducing the nation's international debt or America's role in the AIDS epidemic. They just want to know about my private life. Midget warned me: It won't go away until I do something.*

Abby drew herself tall, ruffled her notes and gave the reporter a steady stare, warning him to prepare for a big blast. *I may be putting my finger in a light socket,* she thought, *but here goes.*

She shook her finger at him. "How dare you inquire about my private life. You have no right. Women are no longer the cheerleaders of life. We make our own decisions. I'm a widow and a mother. I no longer need anyone's permission and most certainly not *yours* to do things. You may not ask those questions of me. That's life, that's real. Get used to it, get on with it, or get out. Next question."

I've probably succeeded in moving the needle of political numbers in the wrong direction. Wonder what the polls will say tomorrow?

"Madam President, what about the downing of the Chinese fighters?"

Abby smiled, then looked at her hands, conveying deep thought. "I've already spoken to that very unfortunate incident. Our pilots didn't start it, but they finished it. Bottom line: Don't mess with the USA. The pilot of the MMA is Navy Lieutenant Bill 'Skinhead' Smalley. One of our fighter pilots is a courageous female Marine, First Lieutenant C. J. 'Pipes' Walston, both very brave Americans. Thank you, ladies and gentlemen.'"

Midget Berry fell in beside her as she left the podium.

"Go get 'em, girl," she whispered. "You're much better when you're angry. Show some grit, belt it out. People like you for getting your whole self out there. A man couldn't do what you just did. I might have crafted a few better lines if I had a heads up."

"Hell, I didn't know myself. It just happened," Abby chuckled softly.

~ **Twelve** ~

Blake sat in the Beijing office of Ambassador Martin Chee, an American lawyer rewarded with the post for his many contacts in China.

"President Steele, hello. This is your admiral on assigned duty. I have a report for you." he shouted. "Do you hear me all right? This secure connection sounds like I'm talking into a seashell, over."

"I hear you okay," Abby said. "Thanks for the call, Blake,"

"I won't take long, but thought I'd give you my initial thoughts. Plato and I haven't gotten very far. Six days and we're still waiting in Beijing."

"What seems to be the problem?"

"I'm no longer on active duty and just a retired admiral. So far my 'special envoy' title hasn't gotten their attention. But then, these people have their own agenda."

"Has Ambassador Chee been helpful?"

"My meeting with him went very well. He's cooperative and doesn't appear to resent my being here. However, he doesn't know any more than anyone else. He did say their single-party democracy doesn't work like ours. I tried to arrange a meeting with Colonel-General Zhang Liu, the head of the Peoples Liberation Army, but he wouldn't see me."

"Should you come home?"

"You miss me?"

"Of course. But I meant, if you can't meet with the right people, you might as well be here."

"No, I settled for a meeting with the leader of their navy, Admiral Pengfei Chen, later today. He can see me for only a half-hour. He remembers me from my days as commander of the Pacific theater. I'll report my findings after that meeting."

"Good, could be interesting."

"In the meantime, it would seem that *if* this nation is on a war footing, the common person, the "street Chinese," as you would say, doesn't know it. Nary a hint of it in the newspapers, but maybe not so significant because free press is an oxymoron here."

"I look forward to your report."

"Well, you have my first pound of research about the Chinese. Wish I had more to report, Madam President."

"Goodbye, Blake. Stay safe."

"Goodbye from your humble servant — who loves you."

~ ~ ~ ~

A thousand members of the National Party Congress faced the stage in the Great Hall of Beijing. They waited anxiously for Sun Yuxi to begin his speech.

"You remember the old proverb, don't you?" Sun Yuxi said to the men in the audience. "The most difficult part of a journey of a thousand *li* is the first step. We took that first step in 1949 and again in 1989, and now the reformation is underway. However successful, it has created its own problems. Now we do not import enough fossil fuel to support our growth."

A young member of the Congress shouted sarcastically, "We have too few farmers and too many factory workers. Too many cars, not enough oil. The *danwei* culture is breaking up."

"I say we must fight for our oil," another shouted.

"Sit down. You want to fight everyone all at once," the aging president responded. "Sit down. We must be rational about this."

"Fool," a dissident shouted. "You paper tiger. You never stand up for your country."

"I will match my service in the Peoples Liberation Army with yours. Do not disparage my patriotism," the President retorted. "You are all fools. We will end up fighting the Russians and if we're not careful, the Americans at the same time."

"So? We fight if we must. We need oil," said another young representative.

The president waved his hands. "Gentlemen, gentlemen. Behave," Yuxi shouted above the ruckus on the Party floor. "I will refer this all to the Politburo."

"Ha. What Politburo? Old men, all of them. We need young blood to lead us," a voice shouted.

"New leaders and fight for oil." They pounded their hands on the tables to a four-four beat.

"New leaders and fight for oil," they chanted.

"New leaders who will fight!"

~ **Thirteen** ~

In his hotel room, Blake slipped on a dressing gown over his slacks and took a seat on an ornately-carved oriental chair near the window. A light, sweet aroma of perfumed incense filled the room.

Unaware of the struggle taking place in the Great Hall of the Forbidden City on the other side of Tiananmen, he relaxed with a cup of green tea and gazed across the open square. He saw the mass of people on bicycles and cars moving like busy ants to their destinations.

Looks much like Washington, he thought. *Where I prefer to be, with her.*

He thought about his mission and reviewed in his mind how he came to be sitting in the finest hotel in the capital of China as special envoy to POTUS. *It happened while on a midshipmen cruise in the Mediterranean Sea. I went on a tour of Madrid with Erie, my old buddy from sailor days and, true to form, we ran into three college girls on vacation. Abigail Cass was the standout: Beautiful, smart, a down-to-earth sense of humor, but very independent. During the few days we had together she tried to stuff an arts education under my engineering skin. We kissed, I fell in love, and we promised to see each other again in Paris. I never made the date because the Navy ordered my ship to chase a Russian submarine. We corresponded and I even invited her to a midshipman dance, but she couldn't get away. Our lives took different paths. I married Beverly and Abby married Buck Steele, somewhat older than herself. He took over the presidency of CASS, a small furniture company, from her father and turned it into America's first billion-dollar conglomerate.*

Years later we met again when CASS Corp., a major defense supplier, held a big party in a Detroit hotel and invited several high-ranking military officers. We talked for few minutes and I learned she took over the reins of CASS Corporation due to some sort of shakeup over stock prices.

We met again when Buck had a heart attack and died suddenly — they were in Taiwan negotiating with the Japanese. To talk on a secure net, Abby landed aboard my Seventh Fleet command ship.

It's funny how you bump into people. I went to Washington between assignments — Bev and I were divorced by then – she had taken the kids. I caught Abby's eye in the midst of her campaign for president. I barged right up and gave her a scrumptious hug. That did it for me. Although, right off the bat, she set me straight on our relationship, I whittled her down — got under her skin. God, how I love that woman.

The hotel telephone jarred him back to the present. Blake put down the teacup and answered it.

"Admiral, it's time to roll, sir," Lieutenant Docket, his aide, said. "The car's waiting in front of the hotel. Dr. Wang is ready."

"Thanks, Melvin. I'll be right down." He dressed quickly and joined his traveling companion in front of the hotel.

Passing Tiananmen Square Plato said, "I grew up here, and now, I've shown you most of it. The old walled cities, the Temple of Confucius, the Forbidden City. The big shift came almost immediately after June 1989 and the massacre of hundreds protesting for democracy. Deng Xiaoping, Mao's successor, threw the Chinese people a very meaty bone by opening the door to capitalism and turning loose their entrepreneurial spirit. Beijing, "Peking" in the early days, turned into a modern, cosmopolitan, ethnically diverse metropolis."

"Is this it?" Blake wailed. "What haven't you told me about the Chinese? Six days of wasted time. Tomorrow we're on a plane, no matter what. I'm not staying one more day."

"I agree, admiral."

"And your dissertations about their philosophies have not been lost on me," Lawrence growled. "But what will I think when I meet the admiral?"

"Well, sir, we need some indication why they deployed their forces. Is it for training or invasion?"

"Tell me something I don't already know," His lips curved into a slight smile.

Plato drew back, unsure of the admiral's seriousness. "All right, sir. This will take my Ph.D. hat." His hand tipped above his head as if he held one. "Here's something you may not know. The Communist party with its top-down management is determined to hold onto power. China has lots of people who make up a highly educated technical elite, but they have a serious shortage of resources, and they have terrible pollution problems. Their ebullient entrepreneurs are straining against outdated and inefficient state-controlled industries. They resent the past exploitation by both the western powers and Japan and are now in a period of resurgent nationalism."

"What does that mean to our mission?" Blake asked seriously.

"We tread carefully."

"Hmm." Lawrence's brow wrinkled. He looked at his hands and nodded.

"Should we be scared or encouraged?" Dr. Wang shrugged. "Well, let me answer my own question. China should not want war since they are now making real gains. The middle class has grown rapidly, and they have raised their real income. But they feel their oats. I think they need to know there are limits and what those limits are."

As the car sped to the headquarters of the Peoples Liberation Army, Blake saw long lines of private cars at gas pumps, military trucks and tanks moving north, and a mishmash of activity. At a public pool, women dressed in the latest swimwear and men played mahjong. People in Ralph Lauren jeans and Gucci ties came out of a Starbucks and a McDonald's. He saw traffic jams and heard the taxi and bus horns blare. The endless building of skyscrapers, high as stars alongside a statue of a fat Buddha, told the dichotomy of China. Within ten kilometers of all that modernization, the view changed to abject poverty and squalor.

What do they want? Probably what they see on CNN and the movies — what we have. They love to gamble. It's in their blood, but are they willing to gamble away their opportunity?

Blake reviewed his own assessment of the country's military. *The PLA has seventy-five army maneuver divisions compared to America's ten. The 15th Airborne Army has three divisions ready to act as a quick reaction force. Their Air Force has more than 400,000 personnel and about 4,500 combat aircraft. Their Navy has over 160 mostly-modern seagoing ships, and they've expanded and modernized their submarine fleet. In addition, they've built a nuclear intercontinental ballistic missile arsenal and pointed it toward the United States. If we went to war, what a hell of a fight!*

The car stopped. A Chinese officer held his door open. Blake exited and walked to the curb to greet his old acquaintance.

"Admiral Pengfei Chen."

Blake warmly clasped the hand of the senior naval officer of the PLA, a man, once slender but now paunchy. He wore about fifty medals on his left breast, a result of long service but little war fighting.

"Admiral Lawrence, welcome back to China."

Still holding Lawrence's hand, Admiral Chen bowed. "Good to see you again. Come, we'll go to my office. Tea?"

They walked side by side past soldiers rendering salutes to Admiral Lawrence. A band played march music. They strode through the foyer where other senior officers stood in rows of welcome, then into a large, open office where a sofa and chairs surrounded a low table.

"Please," Admiral Chen motioned Blake to sit and took a chair opposite him.

Blake noticed no photographers and other media people usually present for internal publicity. *Looks like I'm not a front-page visitor.*

A mixture of old and new China patched together like a gift pack of different colored beer cans filled the room. Beautiful rosewood tables sat near computers and chrome-legged chairs.

They spent the first ten minutes in pleasantries, sipped green tea, and talked about family, children, and sports.

An aide came to Pengfei Chen and whispered in his ear.

"My scheduler advises me I have another engagement shortly, Admiral Chen announced. "Admiral Lawrence, to what do I owe this honor?"

The son of a bitch. Blake thought. *More of it. A breach of respect or an attempt to avoid the subject he already knows.*

"Sorry about the scheduling, Admiral Chen, but I was under the impression you had more time. I'll get right to the point, American style." He feigned a smile, knowing Pengfei Chen understood American culture better than he knew China's. "It's about the deployment of your naval forces. We know you ordered them out of home waters and into the South China Sea. Your country took possession of the Spratlys and had an altercation with our air forces. Now your naval armada approaches the Straits of Malacca near Singapore. What's the reason? No one in our embassy, not even the military section, has a clear picture."

Chen's large protruding eyes bulged even more, then blanked, his expression stoic and unchanging. "Oh, that. Just a friendship cruise. Not unlike those we have sent to your country, even to South America. No, I don't think America needs to know anything special."

"All right, I'll be blunt. I've been sent here to convey a clear message to you and your government. The movement of those naval forces could be dangerous."

Chen jerked alert, but his facial expression remained bland. "What do you mean?"

The cat and mouse game, Blake thought. "We are also aware of the possibility of a war between China and Russia over a boundary that affects the Pan-Asian pipeline and that your country may strike out to secure oil by force."

"What makes you think that?" His face remained unchanged.

"We know a great deal, sir."

"You need not worry, Admiral Lawrence. History shows we are not a warring nation. Besides, we are weak, not strong like you. We are a poor third-world country struggling to care for our people. *We* have a population of over a billion. What concern is it of America?"

Don't try that old stuff on me, Blake thought. *Weak? Like hell.*

"Admiral Chen, if you disrupt the traditional flow of fossil fuel, you may force the United States to intercede. We will not tolerate military operations that interrupt freedom of the seas."

"Like what?"

Blake's eyebrows arched. "Like, we will fight you."

"For what reason?"

"Admiral Chen, you know the reason. Freedom of the waterways. Other countries need oil as well as China."

"You have a woman president. Women have too many feelings. She will not fight."

Blake's chair skidded back with a screech across the tile floor. He stood to leave. His jaw tightened and face reddened. He drew himself to full height and towered over the Chinese man.

"Maybe Chinese women have too many feelings, but I can assure you your government should understand I am the personal representative of President Steele. I know her. She sent me her simple message. 'We will fight." He breathed a sigh. "I hope you and I don't have to meet in a sea battle."

~ **Fourteen** ~

With Plato in tow, Admiral Lawrence returned to the White House to give his report to Abby together with Wilmer Flanagan, Reed Alseño, Bull Mullin, and several high-level staffers.

"The country has modernized, causing significant energy shortages," Blake said. "However, all the top-level people have gone silent about their military movements, and they seem to be very sensitive to American interest."

"Meaning?" Abby asked.

"Maybe it was the bombing of their embassy years ago or the Taiwan issue. Not even my old acquaintance Admiral Pengfei Chen would divulge anything. It's like everything has a 'top secret' label."

"To what do we owe this?" Abby asked. "Dr. Wang, what's your opinion?"

Plato bowed. "I didn't hear anything either, but I traveled with a high-level person. Truth is, they don't trust the simplistic ways of American culture. They think we're too much into other people's business. They believe what they do is none of our concern."

"But why in the hell so secretive about moving naval forces into the South China Sea? Did we find that out why?"

Lawrence and Dr. Wang shook their heads. The others stared blankly.

"We know no more than before," Blake said. "They'll tell us in due time. In other words, when they're damn well ready."

Plato nodded in agreement. "We may need spies inside."

"Hmm." She stroked her chin. "Thank you, gentlemen, I'm still at square one." She rose to her feet and said dismissively "Get me more information."

While the men left in single file, Abby called Blake aside and whispered, "I'm too busy to spend time with you just now. Would you mind waiting for me upstairs?"

He smiled, scratched his head, and agreed.

He made an excuse and exited toward the West Wing, then changed direction and went up to her living quarters. *What a change! Once commander of all naval forces in the Pacific, now I'm just a dancer to a woman's tune. On the other hand, while I don't mind dancing to her tune, I do mind having to disguise my comings and goings from the White House. Frankly, I'm tired of playing cat and mouse with the media and the paparazzi always at work. And now Anna suggested the other day that I should stay away except to escort her at official functions. I understand Abby needs someone near whom she can trust and can get below the radar. Abby's like that. For her, it's all about trust. I guess her years in high places taught her about bureaucrats. Let her down once, and you're dirt.*

Blake took a book from his briefcase and found a comfortable chair. Whisper sprang onto his lap. He settled in with a book to wait for Abby. *I'm glad I overheard the White House staff writers. They said to understand President Abigail Steele; one had to understand Jane Eyre.* His fingers caressed the rare first edition.

The sun careened off the windows and lighted the pages of his book, then dropped behind the branches of the freshly budding trees. Blake closed his eyes. Soon his head bobbed and tilted such that his chin rested on his shoulder, and he drifted off for an afternoon catnap.

~   ~   ~   ~

"Blake," Abby whispered. "It's time for supper. Hungry, darling?"

His eyes opened, and he grinned broadly like a child, bright and ready. He reached for her hand. "Give me a minute, woman. Let's see, where's the head? Mouth tastes like rotten fish."

"Hasn't moved anywhere the last I looked." Accustomed to the Navy nomenclature, she pointed in the direction of her personal bathroom.

On his return, he held her chair, then slid into the other at the small, intimate table prepared by the White House staff.

"Hmm, I'm starved," she said, then to the waiter. "Thank you, William." He retreated out of earshot.

"How'd your day go?" Blake asked.

"Never changes. I run from one fire to another. Thank God for the good people around me. By the way, after you left, Wilmer read a couple of dispatches he received from our Chinese embassy. You got good reviews for your trip. I see you killed time reading. *Jane Eyre*?"

"Of course. You know it?" he asked.

"Required reading... in the tenth grade, maybe? No, in honors at Barnard."

"Speaking of Barnard, how's your granddaughter doing?"

"Oh, Third. I seldom hear. She's so busy. She must do well, but Anna doesn't say much about Third and Barnard. You'd have to go to the school to understand what happens there."

"I know what happened to you. Remember when we first met in Madrid?" Candles splashed shadows across their plates. He reached across the table and touched her hand.

"You fell in love with my lips and anything else you could touch."

"Well."

"You never told me about all your loves as a midshipman. I know about your ex-wife, but there must have been more."

"Only one besides you. Viva Voce. Real name Kathy Velenochi."

"Viva? The famous singer? The movie star? How did you meet her?"

"Through Sam. After an Army/Navy game in Philly."

"What happened?"

He shrugged, "She went to Hollywood. That was that."

"Beverly. You seldom mention her."

He shrugged again. "Didn't work out."

"Why did you marry her?"

"What are you? The girlfriend police?"

"Just nosy, that's all." She squeezed his hand.

"She'd already graduated from Vassar when I met her."

"That liberal all-girl school. Like Barnard, but not as good."

"There you go again. Miss Snooty."

"What was she like?" Abby asked.

"I've told you before."

"Tell me again."

"My, what a nosy mood. She'd already started her own career in merchandising. For me she stood out in a crowd, slender and aristocratic. She wore tasteful conservative but modern clothes. The quiet kind who would go braless to show her independence."

"More. Fascinating," Abby said.

84

"You mean high-schoolish."

"So? Tell me more."

"When I asked her to marry me, she told me the Navy seemed too narrow for her. She distrusted the scope of the military mind, too confining. She said she had never met a military officer who had read anything literary, let alone understood it."

"Sounds familiar. Go on." Abby chuckled.

"Beverly wanted to continue with her career. She wanted to delay our marriage until I finished my required service and left the Navy."

"You knew that wouldn't happen, I bet."

"Nevertheless, we married the year after I graduated. She agreed to the marriage only after a romantic weekend in the Bahamas. Four years later, when I wanted to stay in the service instead of starting a business career, she went along."

"Why did it end?"

"Away too much and we grew apart."

"How sad. You must have become lonely over the years."

"Some. It's okay now." He looked away.

"How are Blake and Martha?" Abby rang the dinner bell for service.

"They still live on the coast. Would you believe Blake's two boys are big? Martha's kids are doing well also."

The waiter cleared the table, exchanged presidential dishware for presidential snifters filled with Drambuie and coffee. Finally she told the staff to leave them.

Alone, their conversation came easy. The two agreed they lived lives only written in novels and laughed at themselves: She, the daughter of a wicked drunk and he, the son of a naval officer who left his family to marry a younger woman.

The candles' glow highlighted her auburn hair, tied back in Spanish style just for him. Lawrence mused, *she still looks the same to me. Maybe "the maker" planned it this way, vision fades as the wrinkles grow.*

"Here's looking at you, kid, Humphrey Bogart in *Casablanca*." He held out his glass and touched hers.

She made an impish face that transformed her chief executive manner to coquettish.

His heart pounded and he felt other things happen in other places. His fingers caressed her cheek. "You look lovely."

"Thank you, sir," she purred.

Like a couple of kids, their eyes met. She put her hand over his, which still rested on her face. She took his palm to her lips and brushed the lines, then kissed a finger.

"We could dance, if you like," Blake suggested.

"Put on the music." Her eyes brightened.

They rose in silence. He held her chair then put on her favorite, Julie London's rendition of "A Foggy Day in London Town." He took her in his arms and they swayed to the rhythm. He leaned over and kissed her neck. She twisted her head back and forth slightly and made a sound not unlike a cat. He undid the ribbon and her hair fell down her back.

As they danced, the music segued to their other favorite singer, Frank Sinatra. His voice crooned "The Lady is a Tramp — Summer Wind — Strangers in the Night," and finally "What Now, My Love." His hands moved to the curve of her back and then lower. She cupped hers across the back of his head and melted to him. Their bodies moved as one, floating in their private ocean.

Silently, she took his hand and led him toward the bedroom. Docile, eyes following her, Lawrence felt an excitement sensed only with her. Their passion rose until they reached the throes of ecstasy.

"Tell me it can't get any better." She clung to him.

"No one knows what life can bring. Marry me, Abby."

"Oh, please, I can't deal with that right now."

"Why not?"

"It's better this way."

"Like me sneaking around to be with the president of the United States?"

"You'll survive."

"Maybe," he pinched her.

"Stop that. No, don't. I'll think about it. I'm not sure I'm ready to leap into love again."

"Don't think too long. You know what happened after Madrid..."

"Yes, then *you* went to sea, and I found another man." She drew circles with her finger tips through the hair on his chest.

"You have me going off to Russia in a few days."

"You'll come back to me."

~ **Fifteen** ~

The next morning Abby picked up Whisper and slid into the chair behind her desk; she pondered the stack of papers waiting for her signature. She looked at one then put it down. Her mind wandered. *Blake will soon board a plane for Russia. Each time he travels I feel the same sadness I had when we lost Buck.*

"Focus," she prodded herself. "Center your entire attention on the work at the office and the China problem."

She picked up one of the several papers arranged neatly on the desk. As a speed-reader, it only took her a few minutes. It told the whole story of world resource shortages, and not just petroleum. *Earth seems to be running out of everything except greenhouse gases. We have to do something before it's too late.*

Another file held a study she requested to help her better understand the Chinese government. It gave her more background on the country's oil problem and other border disputes. The next document came from a larger folder about America's military weapon capabilities, her continuing education on warfighting. *Can we make progress on any of the other issues plaguing the world if we continue to kill the population by waging war? Can killing solve the shortages?*

A light knock on her door caused her to look up. Betty Porter held another folder.

"More papers?" Abby asked.

"Sorry to interrupt, Madam President, but this just came over from the Pentagon. Thought you'd want to see it right away."

"What is it?"

"It's sealed, but I think it's the new generals list."

"Leave it," she told Betty, dismissing the Navy commander with a nod of her head.

Abby then finished a few more papers, but before she read about the threat of a Chinese military concept called 'Assassins' Mace', curiosity forced her to peek into the Pentagon folder marked "President's Eyes Only."

She skimmed over the letter that explained the Army's selection and chain-of-command review processes, then ran her finger down the list looking for Murphy's name. She read the letter again, looked at the signatures on the reviewing chain then checked the list one more time. *No Murphy Perks. Could this be a mistake or because he's black? Surely not. We're past that in America... aren't we? Why isn't he on it? Several people who knew Murphy told me he was a shoo-in for promotion to brigadier. Should I interfere with the process? Could someone else have tampered with the list?*

I remember my concern when Anna first told me she dated an African-American West Point cadet. It shocked me a few months later when Anna said she wanted to marry Murphy. Over time, I came around to the fact that skin color didn't matter. Murphy Perks, with his Irish-sounding name, came from a fine Boston family of doctors and lawyers, the first to make the military a career. Anna married him shortly after he graduated from the Point.

Her eyes scanned the list again and saw Bull's initials. He knew how I felt. Now he's done it again. Is he testing me? Well, I know what to do about Murphy — but as for Bull? I'll have to play it out.

Abby called her military aide, who never left her own desk until the President retired to her quarters. "Betty, please send for Sam and Plato. Also, if Admiral Lawrence hasn't left for Russia, please have him call me. Then you need to close up and go home. I'm moving upstairs."

~ ~ ~ ~

That evening Abby sat in an overstuffed chair reading while Blake sat across from her with a small pointer in his hand. He told her about guns and rockets and about China and the Pentagon. He laid out charts on a long coffee table with the focal points of China, the South China Sea, and the Indian Ocean.

Blake stood to meet Sam and Plato as they entered.

"Sam. Good to see you. Staying out of trouble?" he asked as they clasped hands warmly.

"I'll never tell." Sam flashed a smile. "It's my story and I'm sticking to it. Gotta catch me first. What's this with the ascot?" Sam's powerful fingers reached up and touched Blake's throat. "Since when did you take to the dapper-dandy fop look?" He held his old Annapolis roommate at a distance as if studying him.

"A new me, you rascal," Blake responded, a bit embarrassed that Sam's good-natured, irreverent ribbing made so much of his new style. "Got tired of navy blue with gray slacks. There's got to be more to life than blue."

Sam pointed toward his companion, "Madam President, you asked me to bring Plato."

Plato gave a slight bow. His paunched belly spilled over his belt buckle, and his shaved head gleamed from the lights.

"Yes," Abby said. "Dr. Wang, you briefed me on the resource shortages and the China situation. I need more help."

"How can I serve?" Plato said, rubbing his eyes.

"We face a possible war with China. Please sit down," she responded softly. "I have an assignment for you, I think. Plato, can you get inside and find out who wants this war? Is there a power struggle? If so, who's it between? Can you do it? You speak Chinese, don't you?"

"Get inside or find out all those things you asked?" Plato asked.

"All of the above," Abby said, smiling.

"Do I know Chinese? How about this? English: He's cleaning his car. Chinese: Wa Shing Ka. English: This is a tow away zone. Chinese: No Pah King." Plato's face remained bland, serious, without a smile.

Abby looked at Sam again and said, "What's this?"

"It's just Plato's sense of humor, ma'am," Sam said. "He's known as the expert on Chinese culture and history, but he's also known as a jokester."

"Ah, I get it. Wa Shing Ka. Washing car. No Pah King. No parking. That's not Chinese!"

An impish grin spread across Plato's face. It grew to a full kick-life's-ass kind of smile as he told more of his Chinese jokes: "English: Your price is too high! Chinese: No Bai Nut Ding! English: Your body odor is offensive. Chinese: Yu Stin Ki Pu."

"Okay, okay. Enough nonsense. That's not politically correct, you know," she said behind a toothy grin. "But, I guess we do need to retain our sense of humor even under these serious circumstances."

"Now, I can't tell you everything we're doing," Abby continued. "It's too sensitive. If you got caught spying..." She paused for several moments. "Diplomatic relations *are* at the edge, and *we* move carefully, but I need more information. Do you have a family, Plato?"

Plato bowed and, in a serious tone, said, "Of course. One wife..." He smiled and said, "and three children, two boys and a girl."

"Where are they?"

"We live in Falls Church."

"Plato, this is voluntary. You need not accept this assignment," Abby said.

"I'll take it and do my very best, Madame President."

"Thank you, Dr. Wang."

She then turned to Sam and Blake. "Would you two please stay for a moment after Plato leaves? I need your advice about the new generals list."

~ **Sixteen** ~

Anna shared a workspace just off the Oval Office with Betty Porter and Margarite Wellaby. Low dividers partitioned the room. From there she often watched her mother make television and radio addresses to the American public and the world.

The week Admiral Lawrence returned from China, he paid Abby another visit on a Saturday night.

The next day the headlines exploded.

Another liaison between President and Admiral

Anna took the papers to her mother.

"What do you think you're doing? I told you this kind of scandal could sink your presidency, Mother."

"Oh, pooh. He just came to brief me about his trip to China."

Anna turned on the television to WDCN. A newsreader showed a photo of dapper Admiral Blake Lawrence leaving the White House. Under the caption the time showed 7:30 a.m.

The accompanying comment said, "To shore up her image, President Steele has shielded herself with First Daughter Anna, who is married to an Army brigadier general. They have three children."

"He's not a brigadier general! My God, Mom. Do they *ever* get anything right?" Anna exclaimed. "He'll probably never be now. The Army will crucify him for puffing his rank."

"Calm down."

"Well, how do you think this will affect your grandchildren?"

"You mean Blake?"

"Yes," Anna said.

"Oh, they'll live through it. Give their pals something to talk about in school."

"Mother, you don't mean that."

"Of course I don't, darling. But what can I do? He does escort me to my dinners, and he goes with me to official visits. I don't portray him as more than a friend, and that's somewhat true. Anyway, I sent him off to Russia this morning."

"Good, a few changes in escorts might distract some attitudes." Anna arranged substitutes to escort her mother to official dinners and accompany her to various functions.

One day the nurse at the hospital where Richard worked tried to get through to the president, but Anna took the call. "Richard's gone off his medicine and we think he's having a manic episode."

"Where is he? Can I talk to him?"

"That's the reason I'm calling. He hasn't shown up for a week."

When the call from Secret Service revealed they'd lost track of him, Anna called Richard's doctor. She even invoked the president's name when he claimed to be too busy to come to the phone.

"Dr. Jones."

"Doctor, this is Anna Steele Perks, daughter of the president. I'm told that my brother, Richard, is missing. What happened? I thought he was all right as long as he was on his meds."

"Can't make him. I'm both a colleague and his doctor. He tells me he takes it regularly but... "

"Any idea where he is?"

"Yes, we think he is in his car driving through the West. He calls occasionally from his cell phone, but he keeps moving. We're worried he intends suicide."

Anna's heart jumped. A bead of sweat came to her forehead and she closed her eyes for a moment. The words formed. "My God, suicide? Why didn't you call us immediately?"

"Well, he sounded like it to me, but... he's a doctor," Dr. Jones said.

"Okay, thanks," she mumbled. "Please call us here at the White House at this number." She read it over the phone. "The president would like this kept as quiet as possible."

"Of course," he responded.

Anna sat back in thought. My goodness, what a life my mother has. Must she now deal with a son having a manic episode who is lost somewhere in the blur of America? This I can help her with.

~ **Seventeen** ~

President Steele and Anna huddled by a telephone in the Oval Office. "You're sure he's not been kidnapped?"

"No, the Secret Service is certain of that," Anna said. "He just ran off — been gone for days. Not sure he'll talk to anyone, Mom, but here."

She handed Abby the phone and punched the speaker button.

"Richard. This is your mother. How are you, dear? Where are you?"

Abby closed her eyes and listened as a stream of foul language spewed from the speaker.

"Richard, listen to me. Please. Just for a minute." She picked up the handset and shut off the speakerphone.

"They're coming in November, November, November. They're coming — just wait, you'll see. Fuck the hospital, they'll see. I don't care. It works. It will save millions. Universal health, education, food, shelter. It will save millions. November, November. It's in the air. Must save earth. November, November."

"Please, darling, tell your mother where you are. Please stay on the telephone with me. I want to help you. Tell me, dear. Where are you?"

"November, November, November. They're coming. It will save millions. Universal health, education, food, shelter, the environment. It will be over then. November, November, November. Got to go."

Then silence.

Abby looked at her phone, then dialed her son's number again. It rang six times before switching over to his voice mail.

"Richard, it's me, your mother. Please contact me. Ask anyone to put you through to the White House. Let me know where you are, and I'll come to you. Please." She gave the number, saying each digit slowly.

She looked at Anna. For a second her head slumped and shook from side to side; a tear glazed her eyes. She straightened up. "Anna, keep trying, will you? I must get back to a meeting. If anything happens, call me right away."

Anna hugged her mother. The two stood with their arms around each other. "I will, Mother."

After her meeting Abby returned to the Oval Office. On top of the papers on her desk was a printout of an e-mail from Blake.

From: Admiral Blake Lawrence, U.S. Navy (Ret)
To: POTUS
Subject: Assigned Duty, Russia

Dear President Steele:

The small piece of land between Mongolia and Kazakhstan remains the only part of original Russia that has not been recovered. For Russia this dispute is about history. For China it is about oil.

Unlike China, where I had to wait six days to see one of the leaders of the PLA, I have already seen every person with any power in this country.

I even met with a few who are no longer in power; primary among those was Mikhail Gorbachev. My observation is Russia has changed. The market is working the magic Adam Smith predicted.

My persuasive powers have been minimal. The Russians are determined to proceed. However, Ambassador London Beaumont thinks there may be some negotiating room downstream. He does think there will be a war over the boundary. Unlike China, where everyone was silent and obedient, here there is an undercurrent that Russia should forego that piece of land rather than get bogged down like they did in Afghanistan.

More on my return, soon.
Your humble servant.
Very respectfully submitted,
Blake Lawrence, Admiral, US Navy (Retired)

She read the next paper titled, "Shen Zhou 3: China's Manned Space Flight Program is Successful."

The next one was her homework about their military titled China's Latest Capability to Shoot Down Satellites.

Finally she pulled her journal from a locked drawer and began to write.

Richard wrestles with his demons, the Russians are about to attack China over a sliver of land, the Chinese may take a strategic island. Their pilots lose all sense of reality and shoot at our surveillance plane. We shoot back and... What next?

What is my real job? I think it's to preserve what being an American means — to serve the American people, helping them to have better lives. Or is it banging back and forth from wall to wall, world problem to world problem? Then there are the poor, the victims of the AIDS epidemic, and macro projects to solve resource shortages. What to do first? And those who make significant achievements need recognition: Scientists, artists, politicians — can't overlook politicians. Am I the only one who cares? I should be with Richard, but... is mothering ever over?

She dropped the book into the drawer and turned the key.

At that moment, Anna burst into her office. "Mom, we have a lead on Richard."

~ **Eighteen** ~

President Steele's destination: Offutt Air Force Base in eastern Nebraska where she would give a major speech about national security. Dressed in a leather pilot's jacket and a ball cap, she strolled across the tarmac. Anna climbed the ladder followed by Betty Porter, who carried the "football," a briefcase containing the president's nuclear weapon launch codes.

Abby then returned the salute of the Marine who rigidly touched his fingers to his cap as she approached. Pausing at the top of the ladder, she waved to her personal staff and a few politicos, stopping by the cockpit to chat for a minute with her pilot.

Capable of flying halfway around the world without refueling, the plane could accommodate more than 70 passengers and included a flying office with covered data systems, secure voice, internet, and other communications.

After hugging Blake, whose plane from Russia hardly settled in at Andrews before he had to scamper aboard for the trip, she made her way toward her chair in the lounge section.

No sooner had she given the traditional thumbs-up to takeoff, the plane lumbered forward; she felt the wheels slam into the fuselage.

She hadn't told her staff, or anyone besides Blake, that Anna had located Richard. A gas station operator near Omaha called the police when he found a stranger sleeping in a Volvo behind a shed just off his driveway. They checked his ID and called the hospital in Pittsburgh, who in turn called the Secret Service.

After notifying her mother, Anna contacted the local media and asked that they not run any mention of Richard or his condition until her mother acted on the information.

Abby's speech, given at a naval base in Florida, was already on her schedule. Citing political reasons, she decided to make it at an Air Force base instead of a naval base. Then she inquired casually if Offutt would be a good location. Her intent was to go to Richard.

As the plane climbed to altitude, she watched an early morning TV news show.

"It's curious the president is giving the speech in such an out-of-the-way location," said the commentator. "With the aid of satellite television, she could give it anywhere; it would get the same coverage and save the public the cost of a lot of jet fuel. Is it fair to surmise that Admiral Blake Lawrence, her companion and maybe more, is along under the pretense of a lesson in what soldiers, sailors, and airmen do? He is the meat of grumblings everywhere from Congress down to the local tavern — the president's inappropriate behavior, having secret liaisons with a love interest. Then again, why is she taking so long to make a decision about China's armada, which this morning moved into the Indian Ocean and is poised to disrupt the sea lanes?"

Abby snapped off the TV. "How do they let that man have a show? He guesses, editorializes, and spreads trash."

Contrary to her daughter's urging not to, Abby brought Blake along in order to keep him out of her closet and show him as a friend and a valued companion. *A man,* she thought, *would not have to go through this — it's a double standard.*

Blake does mean much more to me. The loss of Buck devastated my life. My psychiatrist said work buoyed my spirit and finding Blake got me through the loss.

"Blake, let's get to it. Tell me more about the Chinese military and this thing called 'Assassins' Mace.'"

Blake swiveled his chair to face her and uncrossed his legs. He leaned forward, elbows on his knees. His sea-blue eyes narrowed. "Okay, this is very important — if we ever have to fight the Chinese."

Abby liked him for a lot of reasons; his unpretentiousness and dry sense of humor kept her off guard. Smart, often eloquent and witty, he brought life to her in a way no one else ever could. He made her laugh and feel like she had her feet on the ground.

"It's increasingly evident that the Peoples Liberation Army devotes considerable resources to the research and development of advanced high-technology weaponry in preparation for a conflict over Taiwan. But, more broadly, China could achieve technical breakthroughs that would enable them to potentially exceed certain U.S. military capabilities.

"High-tech programs are not new to the PLA. In '86 China launched its '863 Program' in response to our Strategic Defense Initiative. They focused state research efforts on a range of laser, space, missile, computer, and biological technologies. On New Year's Eve 1999, President Jiang Zemin exhorted an expanded meeting of the Central Military Commission to give him 'Assassins' Mace' to achieve victory over Taiwan.

"This 'Assassins' Mace' concept comes from ancient Chinese statecraft, in which warring nobles sought secret weapons that would attack their enemies' vital weaknesses and bring about their rapid military collapse. In the modern context, the Chinese could use weapons like new supersonic missiles, advanced naval mines, lasers, and anti-satellite weapons.

"Their program follows several years of debate over the relevance of what is called internationally the 'Revolution in Military Affairs,' or 'RMA' for short. Essentially, the RMA posits that advances in information technology, combined with other military technical advances, can give new weapons decisiveness and lethality approaching that of nuclear weapons but without using nuclear explosives."

Abby took off her flight jacket, poured a cup of tea, put in one lump of sugar and stirred. She grabbed a notepad to jot down a few of the facts.

"Since the late 1980s, we've grappled with the concept of RMA, that is, transforming the way our military is structured, how we fight, and with what, and so have the militaries of Russia and China. There's plenty of reason for concern that China succeeded in developing new weapons consistent with the goals of the RMA," Blake continued. "The need to develop an 'Assassins' Mace'" to conquer Taiwan became a clear requirement to turn advanced technology research into next-generation weapons. Evidence appears to support they have done so. For instance, they've harnessed the PRC's burgeoning civil computer hardware and software sector to provide high-tech 'troops' to wage sophisticated computer network attack operations. They can use viruses and other forms of computer network bombs as a means of sowing chaos. Strikes against military communications, intelligence, or command and logistics computer networks could seriously impair a response to a PLA attack."

"So you're saying we might have to fight them with new schemes and technologies."

"Exactly. In the past, military forces have fought with weapons and strategies of the last war rather than current realities. And if this conflict in the Indian

Ocean gets hotter, we have to be ready for anything. Were you briefed that they have a force moving through the South China Sea? The Gulf — Diego Garcia and the Maldives are threatened."

"Yes. But, I don't get it. What is their 'Assassins' Mace?'" What is it?"

"Good question, Abby. Nobody knows. They may have just one weapon that they will rely on – or it could be something that is deployed battle-by-battle. It could be electromagnetic guns, also known as 'rail guns', which use magnets to accelerate a shell to far greater speeds than possible with chemical propellants like gunpowder. There is now abundant Chinese technical literature on PLA research into high-energy lasers, high-power microwave, and electromagnetic weapons. All utilize a form of energy to produce a 'soft' kill that merely renders an enemy weapon ineffective, or a 'hard' kill to destroy the enemy weapon.

"The Pentagon knows they have rockets powerful enough to defeat U.S. satellites. They already have lasers and electromagnetic bombs that produce an intense burst of electronic energy sufficient to fry the complex electronic circuitry in advanced weapons. Delivered by ballistic or cruise missiles, they could render U.S. Navy ships ineffective, and with a minimum of casualties. The next war won't be won by the adversary with the most or the bravest people but the one with the smartest."

Abby held up her hands. "That's enough. Thanks. I'm already saturated with this and all the other warfare material you've given me to study. Let's talk about something else." She turned to Commander Porter and asked her to find Anna and have her come in.

Soon Anna entered with a soda in her hand. "You called, Mother?"

"Sit with me, dear. I just had a briefing by Admiral Lawrence and I'm ready for something different, including our plan of action regarding Richard."

"The car will be waiting. Once you get the handshakes out of the way, we'll slip out. That's it, Mom. I can't tell you what to expect. He could be normal, or he could still be in a depression or even manic. Dr. Wood is coming with us. Besides her M.D., she has a Ph.D. in psychology."

"But Richard doesn't know I'm coming?"

"No."

"Anna, tell me something good. I need something."

Anna thought for a moment. "Well, try this. You know I went with Murphy last month on his first visit as a brigadier in his new inspector general job. What I didn't tell you was while we were waiting in an airport on a trip to Texas, we saw some white people meeting black friends. One of the whites said, as he approached his black friend and hugged him, 'Oh, there goes the neighborhood.' Murphy thought it symptomatic of how much America has changed. That a Caucasian could say that to a black and they sincerely liked each other."

The story brought a smile to Abby's lips.

Admiral Lawrence leaned toward Anna. "So, Murphy got his promotion, did he?"

"Yes, Mom pinned on his stars in her office. The entire family was there plus many of the ranking Pentagon Army officers."

Blake gave Abby a knowing glance; she had exercised her prerogative as commander-in-chief.

~ Nineteen ~

High winds blew hot and gusty across the flatland. Rainless clouds rolled by, white and full, with clean smells from corn and wheat growing tall in the late sun. Exhaust smoke mixed with dirt billowed in the clear late-afternoon Nebraska air behind the line of official cars, then dissipated.

"Mom, relax. He's alive. They haven't moved him. They tracked him through Cincinnati, St. Louis, and finally Omaha, where he apparently came down from the high and crawled into the back seat of his car.

"Hmm." Abby's hands sat crossed on her lap, her fingers moved idly, mothering made her edgy.

Unable to maintain her façade, she excused herself from the hum of the Air Force reception, declaring a needed rest before the evening's dinner and time to prepare her speech. Led by the Secret Service, she and Anna slipped out the back gate of the base and headed for a gas station on the edge of Omaha.

After a half-hour drive, the line of cars, led by state police on motorcycles, pulled into the driveway of the gas station. The owner and uniformed officer met them.

"We took the gun and moved him from the car, ma'am," the officer saluted. "He's in the shed. It's not as hot there."

"Thank you, Officer Brown ..." She read his name from the small bar above his left pocket. "And also, thanks for keeping the media out of this. Anything I can do for you?"

"Lower my taxes," he smiled, then shook his head. "Sorry about that, ma'am, bad timing for a joke."

"I'll work on it."

She and Anna stood outside the wooden shack until the gas station operator, a skinny man named Walker, who smelled of alcohol, pushed the door open, revealing a pile of old mattresses. There lay Richard like a skein of yarn.

Abby walked to his side. The place smelled musty, and the floor was thick with dust and scattered rat droppings.

"Richard, it's Mom," she whispered. He lay facing the wall, and although he was motionless, she could see he breathed lightly. "Richard, do you hear me?"

He moved slightly then turned to look at her through glassy eyes. A dirty fist groped across his face. He rubbed his eyes. A crease formed at the corner of his lips, an attempt at a smile.

"Mom?"

"It's me, dear. I brought my doctor."

"No." He had a distant look in his eyes.

"Please. Tell me how you feel."

His arms were across his chest.

Abby touched his chin, then his cheek, and finally his forehead. She sat on the edge of the mattress and

111

rubbed his temples gently. His face was unshaven, hair uncombed, so different than the clean-cut doctor she knew. Previous episodes had all been in Pittsburgh where he went to bars and downed the mill worker's drink of whiskey and beers called "puddlers and helpers." In the manic state he talked to everyone about nothing and everything, sometimes raging in foul language about his liberal concerns — the world's need for universal health care, education, food, shelter. When he fell into a depression, he stayed in bed, sleeping constantly.

Abby felt pain in her eyes, her brain, and her heart. "Richard, will you please let Dr. Wood talk to you?"

"No."

Abby rubbed his shoulders, then instinctively lay down beside her son. She gently kissed his forehead and stroked his blond hair like a child's. She kissed away his hurt as she had done a thousand times before. Anna closed the door on this intensely private moment, a mother and her 40-year-old son.

A half-hour passed, then an hour more. Abby continued to stroke his forehead, his cheek, and kiss him lightly on his eyes. Her mind stepped back in time, how shy he was one minute and friendly another. How she held him and kissed away a boo-boo after he fell. How she used to listen to his sensitive poetry and read his short stories. How he liked to stay out in the snow and ski long after others had quit for the day. How his brilliance was complemented by how hard he worked in school. How he never complained about anything.

"Richard," she whispered. "It's all right. We're with you. Anna is here also. You're not alone. We love you. Can you sit up, dear?"

Abby sat erect and pulled her son to a sitting position. They sat side-by-side, mother and son, each in tears, each suffering in different ways.

Richard looked at his mother and blinked, then rubbed away his tears. "How did you find me?"

"Oh, someone told us. Do you know where you are?"

"No."

"Omaha, Nebraska. Your car is parked nearby."

"Oh." He shook his head in disbelief and shame.

Abby called for Anna. When she entered the shack, Richard looked away from his sister and shook his head.

"May I let Dr. Ellen Wood talk to you? She's my doctor. She has some medicine that could help."

"Okay. I'll be okay."

"Does that mean you'll let her talk to you?"

"I know what to do for myself."

"You shouldn't doctor yourself. Let her talk to you, won't you?"

"Richard," Anna said sharply, "let her."

"Okay, okay. Get her out of here." He waved a hand for Anna to leave.

Anna opened the door and motioned the doctor to come in. Ellen Wood, a slight woman wearing glasses and a naval officer's uniform, entered. She carried a stethoscope and a medical bag.

Anna stepped out, followed by her mother. They met an avalanche of reporters.

"Madam President, Madam President!" a journalist shouted. "We understand your son is ill. Does that mean you will resign your office to care for him?"

"How did they find out?" She looked at the police officer and then the Secret Service agents.

A camera crew closed in and the journalist asked, "Do you think you can deal with the Chinese now that your son has been diagnosed manic-depressive?"

Another asked, "Is he suicidal? He had a gun, didn't he?"

Anna spoke angrily, without any lisp, "Are you without manners? Have you no decency? No feelings? Come, Mother. Do not answer them!"

They rushed off to their car then circled around back to the door.

"Hurry, get Dr. Wood and Richard into the car. Quickly," Anna ordered.

That evening at the base amphitheater, President Abigail Cass Steele spoke about national security. Her speech had hard words wrapped around the concept of "national interest" for the world at large. She made it clear her beliefs about the defense of her nation should be beyond doubt.

"On the other hand," she stated, "in the global environment of the twenty-first century, all nations' interests spill beyond their borders. America is wealthy and has broad interests, but we see ourselves neither as the world's policeman nor its sole breadbasket. However, we *will* do our share."

She looked out at the audience of mostly military officers, some ranking political figures, and their families. She saw frowns and many nods of agreement. Then she looked at the camera and spoke to the millions of fellow citizens.

"There are two images that should rest heavily with every American. The first is the terrifying image of the atomic bomb. The second, the Apollo 8 astronauts floating through space looking back at the blue marble of earth.

"The first image is one of dread, the other of hope and the possibilities of resolution.

"My vision of peace is a world not always in the shadow of war, but a trusting, yes, a trusting, civilized life for all humankind. 'America,' to use Abraham Lincoln's words, 'has malice toward none.'"

~ **Twenty** ~

When smells changed to Asian charcoal, spices, and incense, Plato knew he had arrived on this island nation across the Taiwan Straits from the Chinese mainland, his birthplace. As a precaution, he entered Taiwan as a citizen on business using his American passport. But on his first evening he met with a group of men in the highest political orbit. They sat on the floor around a low circular table, their legs extended. The room's shades spread a darkness that matched their mood. Serving girls kept their whiskey and beer glasses filled.

He learned through these trusted friends that the PRC had developed an amphibious capability and had amassed 200,000 troops across the channel from Taiwan in Fujian Province. But Plato knew, based on American intelligence, the PRC also had another 300,000 near the Russian border. Each army stood ready to strike.

The slender leader of the Taiwan Independence Party and senior member of the legislative Yuan, Mr. Hsin Chen-hui spoke with quiet restraint.

"We all know how they vaulted ahead in nuclear technology..." he said with agitation.

After downing his glass of beer, Liu Wang, one of the legislator's friends, completed Mr. Chen-hui's sentence. "They stole it from your country. The result of stupid American scientists and businesses supplying advanced knowledge. It has all served to increase the concern for security of the people of the Pacific Rim."

"What's next?" Hsin Chen-hui asked. He adjusted black-rimmed glasses set on a large nose. "They acquired Hong Kong from the British, and they took back Macao from the Portuguese. We'll be next, against our will. They already consider us their twenty-third province."

Wang turned to Plato. "After us it could be America."

"Precisely why I am here," Plato said. "I responded to your invitation, of course." He took a sip of beer, smiled at the girls who moved about serving them, then continued. "They have a few nuclear weapons with long-range capability, but would they use them?"

"They're more of a threat to Asia, but they fear America's retaliation," Wang said. "Hong Kong and Taiwan are such economic models for them that I doubt they're willing to throw that away for a senseless war."

Hsin Chen-hui said, "We need a strong ally, but we must use caution. We need America because many Taiwanese remain distrustful of Japan. They remember that nation's long occupation of Taiwan. Consider the activities of the mainlanders in the Spratly Islands. They laid claim and have a garrison of soldiers there. Their naval force protects them from counterattack. We know about your fighters shooting down some Chinese planes. We could be forced to choose sides."

~ ~ ~ ~

Using only his Portuguese name, Plato Perestrello, he entered Macao, the oldest European settlement along the Chinese coast.

Chao Lin-Kang, his long-time friend, reminded him. "Since 1999 we belong to China; Macao remains only three percent non-Chinese, mostly priests, pirates, and prostitutes. Not a particularly valuable asset, yet I believe it foreshadows China's push to dominate Asia."

Rongji Wah, cousin of the Hong Kong shipping magnate Tung Chee-hwa, offered, "My cousin invests heavily in iron ore as well as scrap. As he says, 'The coming war will require much steel.'"

Plato flew next to Hong Kong, the eighth-largest trading center in the world. There he encountered Anson Chan, a female leader who knew everything and everyone.

"The Chinese are threatening to us all," she said. "As of July 1, 1997, Mainland China assumed sovereignty over the island's 400 square miles and 6.5 million people. Since then a fog of distrust has hung over the place. I think Beijing wants hegemony in Asia."

Plato then visited his friend, Tung Chee-hwa, known as a quintessential Confucian patriarch. A proven manager with an iron fist, a Chinese patriot, a shipping tycoon, and first chief executive of the new government of Hong Kong, Chee-hwa confirmed his large investments in steel. "Your president, Madam Steele, will wilt under the pressure of dealing with the Chinese. Maybe we need more of this or less of that, but iron and steel we will always need and I will have it."

"We are building more Chinese ships for the shipment of oil," Ronnie Yang, chairman of the powerful seven-trillion-dollar Lung Hung Group, confirmed. "The political fight in Beijing for leadership will decide the size of the war, not your president."

~ ~ ~ ~

From the hustle of Hong Kong, Dr. Plato Wang made his way north along the coast of mainland China. The first half of the twentieth century, China held elections for provincial assemblies and national parliament and established a judicial system and a supreme court. Then after 1949 it turned to central control where surly guards checked papers for dissidents and pro-democracy activists. On this trip, compared to the 1960s and 1970s, Plato moved freely. The range of what was permitted had changed enormously. He found the government no longer infiltrated the homes and neighborhoods; children

119

were no longer encouraged to turn in their parents for politically incorrect remarks.

His travels took him to Fuzhou, then west to the inland city of Wuhan, then back east to the coastal cities of Shanghai, Nanjing, Qingdao, Tianjin, all on his way to Beijing. In each of those cities he spent time with people who knew the political undercurrents.

Peter Loo, a dapper young Chinese man who'd established a computer company, warned of the changing landscape in Beijing. "A replacement leader for the Middle Kingdom is being decided."

Plato next sat at Li Yang's table in the kitchen of a typical Beijing apartment. A television across the room sat on a skinny stand. The other modern piece of electronics, a little-used microwave oven, sat next to a wok on a coal stove. His friend's two children studied at a table in one corner.

"Perhaps three wars at the same time," Li Yang whispered, "one with Russia, one with Taiwan, and one over oil. It's ridiculous. We're a land of entrepreneurs and scholars, not soldiers. Chinese should follow Confucius' council to seek wisdom, virtue, and profit, not war."

He thanked his old friend for his hospitality and left. Although dangerous, he wrote his first e-mail report to President Steele.

June 30
Beijing, PRC.
From Plato Wang, Ph.D. Harvard

To: POTUS
Subject: Report

Dear Madame President Steele,

Much has been said about the changes in China since my boyhood, but some things never change. The politics of this nation are very complex. Keep in mind that China is a land of many faces. The search for the new China continues, and because this country is growing so fast, I am getting mixed signals. Here is how I see things so far (I apologize for the scattershot approach and hope this doesn't sound too preachy.)

Here is a summary of what I've learned.

For millennia this powerful and respected 3.7 million-square-mile empire was history's oldest and most populous nation. The Chinese call their nation jong (middle) and hwa (splendor) and regard it as the center of the world.

China possesses vast natural resources and huge foreign exchange reserves and in modern times is making a comeback.

Despite their progress, the Chinese often feel like the global Rodney Dangerfield — they get no respect. Two hundred years of humiliation and bullying from Europeans, Americans, and Japanese, all people whom the Chinese deem inferior, is still in their minds. The reunification of Hong Kong and Macao has inflamed Beijing's obsession to redress these wrongs and recover its national honor.

Unlike Japan, China has seldom aspired to global conquest. Even the Great Wall was a defensive structure. Some here say they are more like Americans: Both nations are proud of their land's sufficiency to support the people, and neither has held a creed to invade their neighbors and seek territory.

But the American attack on the Chinese Embassy in Belgrade, viewed by many as deliberate, fostered anti-American sentiments. The view from Beijing is that the embassy bombing and human rights accusations are symptoms of American's unwillingness to let China play a role on the world stage.

China's quest for oil is its most important issue with long lines at the gas pumps. Taiwan remains the other explosive topic. The island was a part of China until 1895 when Japan annexed it, its first step toward conquest of the mainland. The Chinese remind us, historically, American presidents have affirmed that Taiwan is a part of China. "One China" is American law (Taiwan Relations Act of 1979).

The vast majority of the world's governments recognize Beijing as the legitimate government of China. However, America supplies most of the weapons to Taiwan and treats it as a separate country.

I'm afraid that Sino-American relations are not on a solid basis here. Many believe that the oil highways are about China's survival, and they are ready to fight for that.

With regard to dealing with the oil crisis, I recommend our nation leave no ambiguity about the use of force. Make it clear that our "One China" principle is still in place, and make certain that Taiwan and Japan stay out of the problem.

Many here believe if the twentieth century was America's century, the twenty-first century will be China's. Why? Because the country can dominate simply by its powerful size. It is not clear to me yet but I sense some of the younger leaders want hegemony as this country's foreign policy goal, while some just want predominant influence in the region. Others are fatalistic about this drift toward confrontation and a world war. As in America, there is talk of a clash of civilizations. In America, the fear is called "the sin of statesmen." Those people remind everyone of the German rise before World War I and the failure to arrest the catastrophe that nearly destroyed European civilization.

Both sides need a respite from the febrile mood of the moment. Anti-American nationalism gains momentum in Beijing.

In America a growing consensus says China has replaced the Soviet Union as our main enemy. Doubters of this dominant trend are considered appeasers, acting for their own economic benefit.

Once the die is cast, there will be no easy way back from the precipice.

Your humble servant.
Very respectively submitted,

Plato, the Ph.D., CIA spy, hit the send key. His message flew into the ether of upper space. He knew the e-mail police might intercept and risked his friend's hospitality, so he quickly packed and got back on the road to Beijing.

Vice-premier Wen Chen, who once had less power than the local mailman, huddled with Li Fang and Colonel-General Zhang Liu, commander of the People's Liberation Army, on the top floor of the Peoples Congressional Building. His position among the political powers bloomed after his survey of the Russian border on that look-and-learn trip ordered by Sun Yuxi back in April. This elite group contemplated the astounding intelligence they received.

Wen Chen spoke softly, "A force of American warships sailed from the west coast of the United States. Could the Americans be threatening to dominate the Pacific like the Japanese did during World War II?"

His look-alike boss Li Fang responded quietly. "We must move quickly. We must continue to mobilize but be careful not to alert the American Navy. Does President Sun Yuxi know?"

"Of course he knows," said Colonel-General Zhang Liu. He shook his head. "But he will do nothing."

"We think President Steele has a spy here in Beijing delving into our business," Li Fang said. "It's one more reason to move swiftly."

"Nothing concrete has been found yet," the colonel-general said. "We are unsure about the American Navy intentions. Our own spies in Washington acknowledge they sail for war."

Li Fang pounded the table. "Let them come. We will take the oil we need to survive. Never again. Since 1949, when Taiwan became severed from the mainland, it has remained our sacred mission to achieve reunification. We must get the island back one way or another."

"Do we want to fight Russia and America at the same time?" Wen Chen asked quietly, "What will America do?"

"They have a woman president!" Li Fang said. "The Americans are nothing."

"Don't be too sure," Colonel-General Zhang Liu interjected. "Their Admiral Lawrence spoke with Admiral Pengfei Chen. He said she will fight. They sent their carriers *Nimitz* and *Independence* once before into the Taiwan Straits."

Wen Chen attempted to moderate the discussion. "Don't overlook her. Some say she's like Thatcher."

"Signal our fleet and strategic weapon systems to be on alert," Premier Li Fang countered, "nuclear warheads unarmed for now."

~ **Twenty One** ~

President Steele sat in the Cabinet Room at a long table surrounded by her key national security advisors.

"The sailing of a naval force from San Diego west across the Pacific does not constitute an act of war, Madam President. It's routine, done every day," said Secretary of Defense Reed Alseño. He stood behind his chair with his hands clasped behind at military-style parade rest. He arrived after the others had taken their seats. A bit out of breath, he stuttered, "We just sent the battle groups *Eisenhower*, *Lincoln*, and the new *Constellation,* accompanied by the five cruisers and eight destroyers. There are also four SSNs, attack subs with them."

"You sent three carrier groups?" she questioned sarcastically. "And someone told the press it was to check Chinese expansion? Please sit down, Reed."

"Am I *not* the commander-in-chief? Who gave the order? Who told the press?" Abby extended her hands across the table, palms up.

"Yes, ma'am, I mean no, ma'am, but..."

"But," she interrupted, "you expect me to accept this as less than insubordination?"

"We move ships all the time without your knowledge," Alseño insisted.

Secretary Flanagan nodded his head in agreement.

"Not three battle groups intent on going to war with China, *we don't!*" Abby said. "Who ordered it? I want a name."

Alseño coughed.

Silence.

"Well? I'm waiting!"

"Well..." Alseño hesitated, frowning. "General Mullin did, ma'am. But, as chairman of the Joint Chiefs, he has authority to do so."

"Why isn't he here?" she asked.

"Ah, he's in the Command Center," Alseño said.

"Command Center? Conducting a war? Send him to me! Now. I'll be in my office."

~ ~ ~ ~

Again *at her desk, her mind shifted to the problem at hand. How do I discipline a general? And the senior military officer in the whole damn Defense Department at that? He's a professional, and he's been around as long as I have. Should I ever have to speak to him about overstepping? Has he taken up sides? Allowed himself to become politicized? Truman had to fire MacArthur. Should I be hard or soft? Whatever I do, I must do it carefully. I have to read about it the next day in the media. On the other hand, he's got to know where I stand.*

"Madam President." Commander Betty Porter stood in the doorway. She leaned against the door frame with her head just inside. "Sam Talau wishes to see you. 'Hot button,' he says."

"Send him in, Betty."

"Plato is missing." Sam bolted past Betty.

"Missing?"

"Yes, ma'am. We don't know what's up, but he may have been picked up by the police. If that's so, we don't know where they've taken him. My man in the embassy is working on it."

"Damn, just when I thought I had a handle on this. What can we do?"

"I know what we can't do — acknowledge we know anything about Plato. He's out there, as we say, 'in the cold.'"

"Find him! Pay what you must, but find him." She thought of his family in Falls Church. "I sent him, so he's my responsibility. Alive."

Sam Talau, Blake had once told her, could get things done when no one else could.

"I've got people working on the problem, President Steele. It won't be easy. The Chinese have some tough jails, and their laws are not like ours. But..."

"Thank you, Sam. Keep me informed."

Commander Porter crossed paths with Sam as she entered. "General Mullin present and waiting, ma'am."

"Send him in, please, Betty."

The general marched in. His uniform, with seven rows of ribbons, was a bit disheveled for a meeting with the president. A tight smile with his lips parted in an ellipse surrounded his big teeth.

"You asked for me, President Steele?" His southern drawl oozed overconfidence.

"Yes, I did, General Mullin. I'll get right to it. You ordered three battle groups to sail west out of San Diego. Why?"

"Why? Well, yes, ma'am, I did. Do you mind if I sit down?" he asked. He showed a bit more of his teeth between set lips.

"I do mind. I don't remember giving you permission to sail the fleet."

Lips closed and brow furrowed, he stood at attention in front of her desk like most visitors instead of in an overstuffed chair. "No ma'am, you didn't, but I don't want another Pearl Harbor." A slightly sarcastic grin formed on his lips. "It's why you pay me the big bucks. The Chinese navy has transformed itself into a major regional force that can strike anywhere in the western Pacific or Indian Ocean. I got the battle groups underway so that our Navy would not be surprised, like the Japs did to us in WW II."

"I was told the order you gave was to go to the Indian Ocean and be prepared to fight the Chinese."

"Well, the Indian Ocean straddles one of the world's most important shipping routes. The Chinese are definitely up to no good out there."

"Do you know my options, sir?"

"Well, kick their ass... ah... butts is one way, Madam President."

"Crude, but you got *one* right. I would have thought a West Pointer would have offered me more options than that. As I see it, I can threaten them, or I can use diplomacy, negotiate, boycott, embargo, blockade, or send a multinational force, or I can bomb them with air strikes from an American naval force, which seems to be your only answer."

"Harrumph. Well, I..."

She interrupted. "How to fight the Chinese? Or should we fight them at all? Those are the questions. I think we should turn our naval force away, don't you, general? At least until we know what the hell we're doing?"

Abby stood, her signal to dismiss him.

He started for the door.

"Any ideas how the press got the message we sent that force to take on the Chinese, general?"

He shook his head.

"I'm told it was you."

"Well, my public affairs officer did. He's a good ol' boy." His body language and red face showed his anger. To cap off his anger and resentment, he blustered, "To do my job, I need some leeway."

"I'll decide how much."

If I send men and women to war, I need to have the right person in charge, and it sure as hell's not Bull Mullin. Hmm, maybe Blake can take command of the fleet.

~ **Twenty Two** ~~

During the days following her confrontation with Mullin, Abby met often with her National Security Council. "I know I've said this repeatedly, but we still don't know the intentions of the Chinese," she opened, "nor who or what's behind this. Any news from Plato or the ambassador and his CIA station chief?"

"No, ma'am," Sam spit.

"At least the Russians haven't moved into China yet," Alseño added.

"They seem to be at a standoff," Wilmer said. "Both governments seem in denial of a problem."

"Before the next meeting, I need your thoughts about these questions: *If* America has a war with China, would it be a righteous war? Would an attack on oil-highway aggressors in the Indian Ocean mean a world war? Would our people believe in it enough to make sacrifices, enough to take up arms? What is a righteous war? Is it one that picks the bones of the poor by sending their boys to fight? Is there a correct proportionate response for this scenario? If we enter into it, what is our exit strategy?

"Ladies and gentlemen, as today's witnesses to history and the prime participants, we had better get this right." Abby continued. "The Japanese, South Korean, Taiwanese, and Philippine ambassadors have all called on me within the last week. Most believe China intends to expand and all have the same concern: Will America permit the Chinese to divert oil supplies? I told each of them that when I last met with Ambassador Li, it did not go well. Mr. Li continues to make complaints about the shooting down of their planes. The meeting turned into threatening accusations. Although diplomatically worded, the statement he read said, 'China would consider declaring war if interference in the South China Sea continued.'

"However, when I asked Mr. Li about their intentions in the Indian Ocean, he gave a vague response, 'My country's activities anywhere are none of America's business.'

"The reason the meeting deteriorated was partly my fault," she admitted. "I made statements meant to irritate by mentioning that one of the American fighter pilots was a woman. When he threatened war, I suppose I got on my high horse some. I wanted the message to get back to whoever is running that country: They want philosophy; I gave them philosophy. I explained Americans wouldn't resemble one another even if painted all one color. We speak all the languages of the world and accommodate an astonishing mixture of civilizations. Still, our spirit of solidarity turns on like a choir when it comes to freedom.

"I asked him what he thought would unite Americans. He didn't answer. So I answered my own question: Freedom works such miracles that one should never miscalculate what is truly important to Americans."

"She sure gave him a first-class lecture." Wilmer added. "She told him that America had a worldwide interest in freedom, particularly freedom of the seas."

"Well," Abby cut him off. "Let's get on this China situation."

~ ~ ~ ~

Shortly after meeting with the NSC, Romeo Seward, Abby's political consultant, a prominent member of her party and her primary point of contact, came to warn her of the re-election implications.

"The fact that you have a disagreement with the chairman has leaked. My guess is he did it." Romeo continued, "Anyway, Madam President, it's caused a drop in your popularity. Some members of Congress, friends of Bull, question your leadership. America liked you when you stood up to the press but less when you stand up to a general who has a lot of grassroots popularity himself. People do like him. He comes across as an 'aw shucks,' good ol' boy with his heart in the right place about America. Some already think of him as presidential material and your competitor in the next election. He hasn't run from the rumor. That is *if* you're running? Decided yet?"

"They don't think I care about our country? No, I have not decided. They really think of him as presidential material?"

Romeo's fat, broad hands moved constantly while he talked. The shoulders of his coat showed sprinkles of dandruff, and the buttonholes stretched across his overstuffed belly. "Well, apparently many do think of him that way, but not only because you're a woman. There are many who see you as rich and elite."

"Hmm," she said.

"Then there's this new thing."

"What new thing?" Her eyes jerked toward him. "As if I don't get enough criticism."

"Well, someone — a reporter — nosing around Saginaw dug up your mother's background and the name Monte Carpenter. I know about Lucile, but who the hell is Monte Carpenter?"

She shook her head in disbelief. Her thoughts went to Mullin and his cronies. *Are they trying to stab me in the back? Those bastards! Why now? It never came out before.* President Steele sat back in her chair and looked at the ceiling.

"Do you know something about this man?" Romeo persisted. "I've got to know, or I can't do damage control. Frankly, Madam President, the people are restless. They want an aggressive leader. This will only add fuel to the fire."

A long silence.

Should I comment at all, even to Romeo? It's something I've never talked about, never even admitted there's a concern. The kids... I never thought they needed to know. "They're all dead," she blurted. "Lucile, Big Lew, and Monte. It's no longer a story."

"Want to tell me about it, ma'am? It's all over Congress." Romeo uncrossed his legs and leaned forward in anticipation of some juicy news he would have to play carefully in the party and the press.

"No, I don't. Leave it alone." She looked away and shuffled papers.

"But there are rumors in Saginaw that you are not Big Lew's progeny. That you were fathered by..."

"Leave it alone." Her eyes flashed.

"Okay, ma'am, but sooner or later... I guess it's your prerogative."

"There are many ways to say things without lying," her voice returned to normal from the previous angry pitch. She shrugged. "I'll be good-natured about it if it comes up at a press conference."

"It *will* come up, believe me," he said. "It has to do with who your father is."

She shook her head no. "There are many reasons not to tell everything to the public — finances, health, security of our citizens, security of our soldiers and sailors — a classified operation to avoid hurting the family."

Unsatisfied but aware he wouldn't get any more information, Romeo rose. "With your permission,

Madam President. If you decide how to deal with this new issue, let me know."

She remembered, years before, when Buck said, "Any man can provide sperm, but Big Lew has been your father in every other way, and the question of who provided the sperm for you is still in doubt. Who knows why your mother told you Monte was your father? Maybe she was on the grape that day or she was upset with something Big Lew had done or said. You know she could be a vindictive person."

Abby's mind went back to the last occasion she saw Monte at the Saginaw Club. Carpenter came by their table and paused only long enough to greet them as she and Buck sat having a cocktail. If it ever happened, and it probably did, knowing her mother, Abby could see why her mother might have been infatuated and even had an affair with the handsome, almost-pretty man. He wore a small well-trimmed dark mustache and dressed dapperly. According to rumor, during one of those periods when the Cass family tried to control Lucile and save their name and reputation, she rebelled and did one of her behind-the-scenes capers — the rich kid marries the daughter of a whorehouse owner. He didn't have to marry her, but Big Lew was honorable to a fault.

Abby had pieced together the story. Lewis Cass, on a dare, took Lucile for a ride in his 1918 Ford convertible, and they ended up in the back seat. Her brother was the unwanted result. Lewis and Lucile married, but it was never a happy union. Lucile had a mind of her own and an independent income from the whorehouses her father left her. Although she tried to be a Cass family lady, from time to time she disappeared to be found later in a rundown hotel, slobbering drunk after a night carousing with men half her age. Apparently, her liaison with Monte was a bit more civilized since they met in the better hotels. The rumor throughout Saginaw was that Abby was the product of one of those nights. She never heard it directly until, during a fight with Big Lew, Lucile told Abby Monte was her real father.

It's over, Abby thought. Monte never showed any interest in me, and Big Lew gave me everything: A Barnard education, international travel where I met both Blake and Buck, and eventual ownership of one of the richest corporations in the world. Regardless of my birth, I will never disown Big Lew. It's none of their damn business.

~ Twenty Three ~

One of those precious early fall mornings in D.C. came with a sun that just popped above the horizon creating long shadows that fell across the lawn. Nearby, small birds sang as they flew among the trees. So as not to be seen and photographed by the paparazzi, Abby and Blake sat in an alcove just off the door leading to a small upstairs patio. She had a heavy bathrobe over her nightgown and hair pulled to a bun in the back. He wore a dressing gown with an ascot.

A pot of coffee sat on the small table. Sweet buns and fruit filled several bowls. They sipped occasionally from their mugs. The aroma of Colombia's best filled the room. Abby's lips curled into a slight smile as she remembered the previous evening. *It was good. I do love Blake. I like having him around. He's fun and he's sexy. But is this enough? It's not translating well across America, especially in the South and Midwest. I know he loves me, but is the timing right? Maybe later? After this term is up and I leave the White House?*

She reached across and took his hand. "I never do this, you know."

"Do what?"

"Sleep in," she said.

"You're the president. You deserve it, occasionally."

139

"My mind slipped rapidly to linear — problem solving."

"Let it. But for a while last night, you didn't think once about China," he said with a grin.

"You devil. But it's on my mind now."

Already steeped in the various opinions of her staff, she knew she must come to a decision. If she did nothing, the naval force now in Hawaii, scheduled for a slow training cruise across the Pacific, would force her into a premature decision.

"As I see it, my options are to go it alone by fighting their force with just our Navy," she said to Blake. "Or delay and put together a robust organization made up of Australia, New Zealand, and maybe Japan. I could call in NATO. Its charter was Northern Europe — now it extends farther East."

"But not to China," Blake said. "With the current mood of the European Union, it's doubtful you'll get a vote from them to send a force."

"Why not?"

"Because I think they have not only lost their ability to fight, they've lost their will to do so. Besides, NATO is basically on the ground. This will be a naval battle, at least at first, unless you decide to invade."

"Korea might agree to send a force."

"True," Blake countered. "But Taiwan will stay out of it to keep its forces in a defensive posture in case the Chinese attack across the channel. If that happens, we may have to get into that."

Abby sipped her coffee. She looked into the Rose Garden and then back to Blake. "Well?"

"Well, what?" Blake sounded like a man enjoying the day and not ready to consider international consequences.

"Well, what do we do?" she asked.

"You don't need my help to decide."

"I know. I hate war — you know there are countries, like Sweden, who have not had a war for over two centuries. I know, you military types scoff at them and call them cowards, but they're not. They're smart. But... I've pretty much made up my mind. I want to pull together a coalition force and not go it alone like George Bush did in the Middle East. It'll mainly be an American operation, but there must be an appearance of an allied force. I want at least token forces from Greece, Spain, and Italy, plus as many Asian-Pacific countries as will come in."

"Don't forget the Brits. They're always with us — they'll jump in with good-sized support, but you're not making it easy for the force commander. It would be a lot easier to go it alone — no interoperability problems, no language problems, and no mission crossover problems. The commander of this op better be steeped in collaboration with foreign forces, and very senior. Naval officers understand seniority muscle. It makes it easier."

Abby looked away, then back to him. "Yes, you will be, and I'll miss you."

He looked up quickly. "What's that mean?"

"That means I'm calling you back to active duty to take command of our naval force."

"You're what?"

"Are you refusing your commander-in-chief?"

"Of course not, but there are a lot of younger flag officers who could do this. You're kidding me, aren't you? I sometimes don't know when you're serious."

"Well, no, I'm not joking. And yes, there are very competent flags out there but none with your proven combat record. Besides, I trust you. I need someone who understands the sensitivity of all this — while I'm working to prevent a world war. This will be a case of who's saving face and who backs down, if anyone. I'm mindful of John Kennedy and his problem with Khrushchev and Castro in 1962. It might go right to the edge, and if we must fight, I want it to be decisive and done quickly. We must show that war is our last resort. You'll do this for me, won't you, darling?"

"Silly question." His hand squeezed hers. "Hmm. Back on active duty? Going to sea again." His face brightened. "There is an advantage to being the boyfriend of the president. He stood and walked to the patio door and then to the railing. He looked out toward the horizon as if on the bridge of a ship. He spoke over his shoulder. "I better get my uniforms and sea chest in order. I was just getting used to wearing mufti, but I'm ready for a blue suit."

"Don't stay out there too long, darling," Abby warned. "You'll find your picture on the front page again."

Blake came in and sat down, then stood again. It was as if new energy flowed into his body. He and Abby were both fit. She was a well-made woman, and for their age they were above average — a few aches and pains, backs a little stiff in the mornings, but nothing to prevent him from going to sea. His face turned to the ceiling. As if musing, he grinned and said, "This is a complete surprise, Madam POTUS, but a pleasant one." His eyes squinted at her. "How are you going to square this with Mullin?"

"I'll take care of that. He'll do what I order, or..."

"This will make headlines, big headlines," Blake said. "I can see it now, 'President appoints boyfriend to command naval force', or better yet: 'Admiral lover goes to war.' It's the stuff of grade-B movies."

"Not right away. I intend to send you quietly. You'll join the force near Midway Island. You round them up and move them to a position east of the Philippines. We won't move until you're ready and I complete my negotiations."

"Mark my words: Mullin will be a problem," Blake said.

~ ~ ~ ~

At a quiet ceremony in the Oval Office, Abby read the commission. Blake raised his right hand and, repeating the same oath he had first said as a midshipman, swore his allegiance.

Abby presented him with the commissioning document. For publicity purposes, she shook his hand. After the camera was out of the room, she hugged him.

Nearby, Anna, Murphy, and Commander Porter stood as witnesses to the oath. Also present were the leaders of both houses of Congress, Defense and State, the CNO, and Bull Mullin.

Abby looked around the room before handing Blake an envelope and addressing her guests. "The Oval Office may not be the best place to recall an admiral to active duty, but it will have to do. The envelope I have just handed Admiral Lawrence contains his orders. You all understand that his appointment is not secret, and you know that his orders are to take command of the naval force in the Pacific. He is not to act until ordered personally by me. I wish to exhaust all avenues short of conflict. For reasons I should not need to discuss, I prefer this not be released to the press until Admiral Lawrence is out of Washington and aboard his command ship. Thank you for coming."

As Bull Mullin left the office, he linked his arms with two congressional leaders, one on each side. He started a conversation in a loud, friendly voice that quickly subsided into furtive whispers.

~ **Twenty Four** ~

Torn between being a mother and her work as commander-in-chief, Abby sat huddled with Anna on a sofa in her private quarters. They held hands and stared at each other with red eyes.

"Richard has disappeared again," Anna said quietly. "This time he's driving a new car he apparently bought on the same day as his escape from the Secret Service. He traded in his old car for a BMW with a ragtop and eluded the police, who were looking for the Volvo.

"Is there no hint of where he's going?" Abby squeezed Anna's hand tightly as if it would bring the answer she wanted to hear.

Anna shook her head. "Mom, I've talked to as many people who know him as possible. You know what a loner he is. He has no friends, just work." She sighed. "His doctor told me he thought Richard was on his meds, but he stopped the consultations about two weeks ago."

"FBI on it?"

"Yes. And of course the Secret Service. It's their jurisdiction. But you don't want the FBI to be distracted from their own work. You could be criticized for it — you know how the politicos and press look for preferential treatment. The police have an APB out for him as a courtesy to you. The press will get this sooner or later."

"The press gets everything, darling," Abby said. "Wouldn't it be nice if someone sees his car in an airport parking lot and we find out he took a vacation to the Bahamas or Tahiti? Or what if he was right here in D.C.? Just look outside — it's the most beautiful time, fall colors, a brilliant sun splashing across the District. The founders must have made their decision about the location of the capital during this time of year."

"He'd more likely be in Colorado or Switzerland — some hilly place," Anna smiled. "You know how he likes the mountains and skiing."

"Remember the time when you were kids and your dad and I took you with us to that ski resort in Canada? Where was that?"

"Banff, near the rodeo place... you know, near Calgary," Anna smiled at the same time she choked back a tear, obviously thinking about those days so long ago. "We would ski all day and then Richard would ski as late into the evening as you let him."

Before parting for the mysteries of the day, Anna told her mother they have another problem in the family.

"Third might be pregnant by her aspiring actor. They've been living together. She's supposed to graduate from Barnard in June."

"Oh, poor girl. What will she do?" Abby asked, her sad eyes searching to help her daughter.

"Don't know, Mom. We don't talk like we used to."

As they parted, Abby asked, "Please let me know the minute you hear anything about Richard — and if I can help in any way with Third."

~ ~ ~ ~

Abby submerged her personal anxieties into her political problems. She drove herself to focus, listening intently as her national security team brought her up to date.

"China has launched a new satellite, probably for intelligence and maybe for over-the-horizon targeting. Could be related to their mysterious 'Assassin's Mace' strategy, whatever that is." Admiral Plexico Crocket, her chief of naval operations, reported. "The Chinese naval armada is still in the vicinity of the Spratly Islands, but it has recently been augmented with another jump-jet carrier. Their armada moved into the Indian Ocean and has disrupted shipping."

"Japan has volunteered to send a small naval contingent to join Admiral Lawrence's force," Wilmer Flanagan offered. "Australia, Britain, and New Zealand already had their elements underway for the rendezvous with the American naval force east of the

Philippines. Several European nations have hedged about a military contribution but offered logistics support."

Abby's eyes darted from one speaker to the next as they spat out information in cold tones.

"Admiral Lawrence already passed through Pearl Harbor. He was briefed and is on his way to the battle force," Plexico Crocket volunteered. "While in Pearl he asked the Pacific Command to make ready the amphibious forces. He also asked the Seventh Fleet Task Force, which stayed clear of the growing Chinese armada, be ordered to move east of the Philippines to rendezvous with Lawrence's three-carrier battle group."

"Your proposal to appoint Admiral Lawrence to five-star rank has gone forward to the Congress," Reed Alseño said. "Of course you know this would be the first such appointment since Generals MacArthur and Eisenhower in World War II."

"The press sees it as a big thing," Midget Berry announced. "Bringing Lawrence back on active duty and giving him command of the force. It has stirred the armed forces and the press to speculate that a mass war is about to begin."

"Several members of Congress have already called me and other West Wing staffers," Walter Coons added. "They think five stars should be reserved only for those who win major wars."

"Their discontent has already been leaked to the press," Midget stated.

Abby remained calm, listening attentively, finally getting what she wanted from her staff: Competing voices, choices, and consequences.

"Congress is off-base about that," Alseño chimed in. "The policy needs to be changed. Ordinary police chiefs in America now wear four and five stars on their collars. A real general or admiral should wear at least five. Several senators hinted to me of an investigation of the unorthodox use of the armed forces. And the fact that there had been no mention of a request to Congress for a declaration of war."

Abby drew herself up and spoke. "This is exactly what I want. I couldn't tell anyone — too many leaks. The Chinese know Lawrence was in command of the Pacific and traveled extensively in Asia before he retired. They were reminded of him when I sent him back as my civilian representative. They know he's a master of naval combat. Hell, he fought gallantly in every war since WWII. It's part of my negotiating plan. This must be held close. I repeat, no leaks. I want the Chinese, who have spies all over Washington, to believe I'm ramping up for a bigger war and possibly an invasion. They think I'm a weak woman. Let them grow a bit uncomfortable."

~ ~ ~ ~

As she left the room, Abby was struck by how quiet General Mullin seemed in her presence. He didn't make any reports to her, nor did he comment on any of the operational matters discussed. She noticed his mouth remained shut except for a slight rippling along his jawbone as if grinding his teeth.

I know what's bothering him. First it was the silent confrontation about Murphy's promotion to brigadier general. Then we had our skirmish regarding the sailing of the fleet without consulting me and the leak to the press. I figure the other thing that irked him was my recall of Lawrence to active duty. Then I ordered him placed as number one on the flag and general officers' list with seniority over all. That was followed by my assigning Blake to command the battle force and my proposal to promote him to five stars. I'm sure Bull's major worry is I might remove him from office. He probably suspects I've considered it. But 'til now he hadn't done enough to warrant that. Besides, there have already been hints he might soon tender his resignation to prepare to run for president in the next election.

After she entered the Oval Office, Sam Talau walked in and stood in front of her desk.

She signaled with a nod of her head for him to take a seat where several ranking administration officials had been setting only moments before. He waited patiently until she finished signing a few papers and watched Margarite carry them away.

"Sam, how are you and your family?" Blake had told her of Sam's closeness to his family — parents in Philadelphia, a wife and five children, a growing number of grandchildren.

"Good, Madam President. Mom and Dad are getting on; aches and pains, you know." He broke into one of his patented big-as-the-world smiles. "We now have seventeen grandchildren — no, eighteen. One of my daughters had another baby the other day."

"Wonderful. Well, what do you have? You didn't wedge your way in here without something important."

"A cliché: Some good news and some bad news."

"Good news first. I can use it right now." Abby motioned with her hands like she was raking the grass.

"Plato finally made contact."

"Is he okay?"

Sam nodded, still grinning. "He's alive. We thought he was captured, but he'd gone underground."

"Underground?"

"Somewhere near Beijing. He's been lying low. All we got was a relay through one of our other operatives that he's okay and will try to get a message to you very soon."

"Thank goodness," she said with a sigh. "I guess I can take the bad news now."

As soon as those words left her mouth, Betty Porter came to the office door and pointed to her wristwatch.

"Sorry, Sam, I'm in a hurry. I'm scheduled for my radio talk in a few minutes. Give it to me quick as we walk," Abby said as she passed him to catch up with Betty.

"The bad news is, I've heard about a possible palace coup."

Over her shoulder she said, "Well, that may be good news, not bad. Let me hear more about that at tomorrow's PDB. A coup in China might be a good thing. Maybe it would bring a more democratic country. At least we would know who's in charge. On the other hand, it could be terrible if a tyrant came to power."

"But, Madam President..." Sam cried out. But she was gone to her next event.

~ **Twenty Five** ~

As the makeup people swarmed about the talk show host, Gabriel London of the World Wide TV network watched WNES Channel 22, the local news channel. The young anchor said, "On a global scale, a possible war looms between China, Russia, and the United States. The sequence of events is as follows: The Chinese positioned an army on their northern border near Russia. The Chinese then moved their Navy into the Indian Ocean. An American plane was shot down by Chinese fighters. An American naval force deployed from San Diego started training exercises near the Hawaiian Islands. The Chinese have massed an army poised to cross the Taiwan channel..."

Gabriel saw the World Wide TV's director hold up five fingers of one hand then let each fall as he counted the seconds to air-time. When he gave the thumbs-up, the host introduced the men sitting across the table on his right and left. Wilmer looked like an immaculately dressed tsetse fly compared to the heavyset, somewhat-slovenly German.

"With the possibility of a world war, shouldn't the United Nations Security Council begin discussions? Why are they dragging their feet? Let us start with Secretary Flanagan."

"I must stop you right there and say I disagree with the characterization that the world is headed for a mass war," Flanagan said forcefully. "As a matter of fact, there should be no war at all if all parties will come to the table. But I'll let my colleague Mr. Gloch speak to that."

Gloch, an old hand at the talk show circuit, dodged the question and looked directly toward the camera. "The European Union, soon to be a single nation of 25 states with a single constitution, did meet to consider the implications of the Asian situation."

"What did you learn?" London asked.

"Well, the world money markets centered in London, New York, Tokyo, and Hong Kong see transfers to less risky investments like gold. This concerns everyone. Currencies move in strange ways when money is pulled back to safe shores. Economies shrink and international trade has ground to a slow pace."

"Doesn't that mean the nations of the world have begun to choose sides? Mr. Secretary, back to you, sir."

Flanagan shook his head. His brow wrinkled. "Well, the world is less mono-polar than immediately after the Soviet Union faced off with America in the '70s and '80s when America became the only superpower."

"You mean after the Berlin Wall fell, and Russia was exposed as a second-rate nation with a third-world economy, don't you?" London asked.

"Well, I consider that a rather harsh characterization of Russia," Wilmer responded. "Clearly, now it is China and the United States who are the superpowers. China's shift toward so-called market socialism and the accompanying economic boom of the 1990s and early 2000s brought about an unprecedented expansion of their economy. The country's Gross National Product mushroomed by 13 percent. Chinese citizens not only wanted the conveniences already enjoyed by their newly industrialized neighbors. Now they want to enjoy the lifestyles of first-world nations like Sweden, Canada, and the United States. The questions facing Beijing's planners are how long and at what pace the growth could be sustained. The boom brought not only increased income but also problems and dislocations. Mostly it has brought an ongoing need for more fossil fuel. Inflation followed and prices soared."

"Back to point. Isn't it true the world is choosing sides? Mr. Gloch?"

"No, certainly not Europe. To a certain extent, Asia is. China is the leader. But other smaller nations like Taiwan, Korea, and Singapore seem to be banding together."

Secretary Flanagan interrupted, "Of course, Australia and New Zealand are steadfastly with the United States."

"True, they are strong financially but miniature in population," said Gloch. "They're practically inconsequential compared to the vastly-peopled countries of Indonesia, India, and China."

London leaned forward. "Is it fair that international political journalists spin this story *not* as a clash of wills over who controls Middle East oil, but rather a clash of cultures? Either of you, please."

"I'll take that one, but only as my personal opinion," Gloch said. "According to some tongue-waggers, of course not you, Mr. London," Gloch gave a crooked smile, "that schism has been discussed. Nationalism has quietly grown in countries formerly colonized. Who knows? The Chinese won't change their system of government to a democracy like the United States. For them, their system works. China has one strong political party that mixes market enterprise with socialism, and for them, it has brought an improved life for everyone. China is on the cusp of passing America as the richest nation in the world."

"One last question: Do either of you know anything about this thing called 'Assassin's Mace' that the Chinese are said to have?"

Secretary Flanagan spoke up. "Afraid you're asking the wrong people, Gabriel. That sounds like a Defense Department question."

Mr. Gloch nodded in agreement. "Sorry, I know nothing about the term."

"Speaking about the Defense Department, is it true that there is a serious riff between Chairman Mullin and the President, Secretary Flanagan?"

Wilmer adjusted his tie knot nervously, then spoke to the cameras, "Of course this is not true. We are one solid team."

"Well, folks. That about wraps it up for today. Our thanks to Secretary of State Flanagan and Mr. Gloch of the European Union. I'm Gabriel London of World Wide TV. Tune in again next week for an update on the issues."

~ ~ ~ ~

Abby heard the grim details as she watched the TV debates rage across the networks. As summer faded into fall, it seemed the nations of earth were like a train rolling out of control for a head-on wreck. People worldwide had made up their minds. Signs of world depression, not unlike the Great Depression of the 1930s, were everywhere. Product sales were weak, unemployment was on the rise, and world travel slowed. Members of Abby's cabinet even suggested that the nation begin ramping up for another world war.

Her embassy and CIA station chief in China provided little information. Plato, her spy, had disappeared again, and the Chinese tightened their robe of secrecy.

She talked with the Chinese ambassador several times to find out what his government wanted, but he remained as secretive as the people in Beijing. She again warned him that confrontation with a U.S. naval force would be suicidal for the Chinese navy. Many would die.

Several newspapers ran opinion pieces with headlines such as:

CAN OUR WOMAN PRESIDENT LEAD US IN WAR?

Others picketed outside the White House holding signs that said:

SHE'S A LOVER NOT A FIGHTER

WEAK WHITE HOUSE WIDOW

A WAIT AND SEE WOMAN

Abby carefully considered her position. *Do I have too many feelings, as the head of the PLA told Blake? Are the Chinese counting on that? I wish I knew them better. They certainly don't know me. I still think they don't understand where they're headed. If they really want war with the West, they'll get their wish by challenging us on the seas.*

She slammed her fist on the table. "I guess war is inevitable."

~ **Twenty Six** ~

Fall dropped from the heavens and landed upon America's capital city. Leaves turned color. Mornings brought foggy breath. Until the sun burned through, early frost could be seen across the grassy borders of the Reflecting Pool.

Abby, poised by her speakerphone, said to Anna, who was on the intra-office speaker, "Connect me."

"No, Mom, he's incoherent."

"I'm on... Richard, it's your mother."

"No, no, no, no, no. It's coming. It's coming. In November — that's it. No, no, no, no, no. The fuck'n world doesn't see it. No, no, no, no, no. Doesn't anyone see? Why are people starving? Why are people sick? Why are people illiterate? This rich fucking world. And old people are treated bad, children worse, no shelter, no food? Why do they hate each other? Why? Why? Why? Why? Why?"

Abby picked up a handset, taking him off the speaker. *The rest of the world doesn't need to hear this.* "Richard, it's me. Mom. Listen to me," she spoke over his constant flow of words.

"No, no, no, no, no."

"Damn it, Richard. Hear me. Where are you?" She never knew what to use, a hard or soft approach.

"Why? Why? Why? Why? Why don't the people of the world have universal health care, universal education, food, shelter? We're rich enough. We're rich enough. We could do it. Worldwide! Healthcare, education, food, shelter. Just a little bit. Just a little bit. Not much money. Just a little bit. Just a little bit. Stop the hate! Why? Why? Why? Why? Why?"

Anna came in and sat on a chair across from her. Abby motioned for her to pick up on the other handset.

"Richard, darling," Abby tried to interrupt. "Tell us where you are. Let us help you."

"Why? Why? Why? Why? Why? Gun. I don't care."

"Oh, darling, do you have a gun? Please don't use it, please. Put down the gun. Let me help. I can help with some of the things you're talking about. Come to Washington. Tell me about it. You can help me. Please, darling?"

"No, no, no, no, no. It's coming. It's coming. In November. November. It will come. You must know. Remember November..." His voice faded, as if the cell phone's battery drained. "November. November. It will co... "

Abby turned to Anna. "Have they traced it yet? Where is he?"

"They're working on it, Mom. They think in West Virginia, but no city yet."

"Richard, do you hear me? It's your mother. Don't hang up, I need to hear more about your ideas. You're a doctor. You could help me. Please tell me more. What can we do? Richard, talk to me. Are you there? Answer me, please. Darling, answer me. Do you have a gun? Don't use it, please. It would be cowardly, you know that. Don't do it, please. Talk to me, Richard." Her mind raced. *I have to keep him on the line. What else can I say? I'll try anything to keep him from taking his own life.* "Darling, your father would want you to come home. Let us help you."

She heard a rushing sound through the phone like running water or wind then heavy breathing and the choking sound of tears. *He's manic — maybe a mixed state — in and out? At first, the way he rambled, I thought in a manic state, but now it sounds like crying.* "Darling," she said softly. "I love you. Anna is here. We both love you. Please talk to me. Please."

"Mom. Mom." His voice sounded weak. The rushing sound in the background of the phone remained steady, maybe the battery draining or a waterfall or a train dashing along a track. "Mom, I'm so sick. Mom. Where are you? Mom. I love you, and I miss Dad. Where is he? I want to go to him. He always helped me." His voice trailed as his tears exploded. He choked, and she could hear the kind of crying that sucked air from lungs, swelling and collapsing in heavy breathing.

"Richard, tell me. Where you are? Let me come to you. Let me help."

"No, no, no, no, no. Why? Why? Why? Why? Why? It's shit, shit, shit, shit, shit, shit. It never stops — shit, shit, shit, shit, shit, shit.

Where is he? Why doesn't he do something?"

His crying stopped between outbursts of cursing, then began again. "Help me. Can't anyone do anything? Why doesn't the world have health care, education, food, shelter? We're rich. Rich. Rich. Rich. Rich. Rich. Shit, shit, shit. Rich. Rich. Rich. Rich. Rich. Shit, shit, shit."

And then another noise, not the rushing sound — a popping noise.

"No, Richard! No!"

Abby's eyes pinched closed, tears came with the pain, the swelling of her chest, the jerked sucking for breath, the shaking of her head. She squeezed her fingers into a fist, drove nails into flesh. Her head dropped to her chest. She felt it all across the invisible distance. She could see his torn, sad body. The real image of her only son. Dead.

"Please," her voice burbled into a whisper. "Please, Richard. Talk to me. Please!" Then she put down the phone.

"Take me to him." The tears turned to defiance, denial. "He's not dead."

"We still don't know where..." Anna put her arms across her mother's shoulders and hugged her.

"Take me to him — when you know." She rose. Shoulders rounded, head lowered, she staggered to her private quarters.

Her mind whirled with sorrow, anger, and confusion. *Oh my God, how could he commit suicide?* She ached for him, and guilt enveloped her. *Could I have saved him? Why? Why? What didn't I do right? Where did I fail? Why? What should I have done? Could I have been more of a mother? A better mother? I should have stayed home.* She flayed herself with self-incrimination and self-pity. She lay across her bed. Her eyes burned from the tears that flowed onto the pillow, tears she could not and would not show outside to the public.

She stopped sobbing, stood for a moment beside the bed, then forced herself to walk to the Oval Office. In her chair, she stared at the ceiling and listened to the sounds of the White House servants moving, a hammer, the scrape of a chair across a marble floor, hushed voices. "The weight of this place," she said to herself. "Can I go on?"

~ **Twenty Seven** ~

Anna came to her and said quietly, "Betty Porter's with me. She has something to tell you, but you don't need to deal with it now."

"I know its bad timing," Betty said. "But the pilots are waiting outside. If you're to see them, it has to be now. They're under orders and have to make a plane in two hours."

Anna stroked her mother's shoulder. "Mom, you can't do this now. Let someone else."

Abby got up from her chair and went to the window. "No. It's something I need to do for several reasons. Get the press secretary. Give me a moment."

She met the two Marines as they entered the room ramrod straight. Abby stuffed the agonizing hurt deep inside and put on a cordial façade.

"Captain Walter Billings and Lieutenant Cynthia J. Walston, United States Marine Corps, reporting as ordered," said Billings, the senior of the two pilots.

"Let's see, you're Razor — and you, Ms. Walston, are Pipes. Did I get all that right? Interesting call signs. Tell me about yourselves. Where are you from?"

"I'm from Beaver Falls, Pennsylvania," Razor said proudly, "and went to Penn State and she's..."

"Oops," Abby stopped him. "I like women to speak for themselves. Pipes, and you?"

Pipe's eyes brightened in her excitement of meeting the President and being in the White House. "I'm not bashful, ma'am — just following protocol — seniors speak first. I'm from Davenport, Iowa, and I attended the U.S. Military Academy at West Point, ma'am. We brought you the black box from the P-3 that was shot down by the Chinese fighters."

"Oh?"

"Yes ma'am. You might wish to listen to their last words. Might help you with your negotiations."

Abby motioned for Betty to take it. "Put it on my desk. Well, I'm impressed with your backgrounds and especially impressed with your work as pilots, vertical takeoff and landing planes, no less. That's why you're all here today, to allow me to have the honor of recognizing your bravery against the Chinese in the South China Sea.

"Captain Billings, would you step forward?"

She pinned the blue and white ribbon with a splash of red down its middle onto his chest, just above his pocket. "I hereby award Captain Walter Billings the Distinguished Flying Cross, our nation's highest air combat decoration for the heroism and courage he displayed in a recent operation defending the freedom of the seas for all nations in the South China Seas. The citation contains more details. For our nation, I thank you, and congratulations."

She repeated the ceremony for Lieutenant Walston and when she was finished said, "I've also posthumously awarded the same decoration to Lieutenant Smalley, the pilot of the MMA."

They thanked her and posed with her for the cameras before being shown the way to another waiting press.

After they left, Abby turned to Anna. "Heard anything?

"Not yet, Mom."

~ **Twenty Eight** ~

Brigadier General Murphy Perks excused himself from the meeting and proceeded toward his office in the Army section of the Pentagon. He had other issues like an officer accused of sexual abuse at a post in the state of New York and a theft case in Idaho.

He walked past the men's room door then stopped. His schedule kept him running from one problem to another and he, all too often, found himself pushing on without thinking of himself. His doctor warned him that a 49-year-old man had different physical problems to look after, especially in Murphy's kind of work, digging into the day-to-day irregularities of a massive organization such as the U.S. Army. Heeding his doctor's warning, he reversed his direction and entered the men's room.

Finding an empty stall, he sat down and proceeded, as he often did, to open a file and catch up on some needed reading.

"She's a whore and a bitch! It's time for her to go. I might do her myself," said a voice from a nearby urinal, above the sound of sprinkling water.

"Not so loud, Harry."

The voices lowered to a whisper.

Their conversation caught Murphy's attention.

167

"Five stars? And she recalled her honey to active duty? Puts him in charge of a fuc'n Navy battle group," the first voice said angrily.

"She's fucking him in the White House," the second voice added.

"Ever notice how she salutes getting on and off her chopper? Like Billy-boy Clinton did back in the 90s."

Murphy felt he should cough to warn the speakers of his presence, but the words hit too close to home. He thought, *Army officers probably, and based on their foul language, probably fresh from the field. Navy and Air Force seldom used this room.*

"You going to the meeting?" one questioned.

"Will Bull be there?" The sound of water flushing covered the next few words of the whispered answer.

"... majors and above, some general officers."

Murphy tried to see through a crack near the hinges of the door without success. *Damn, I know that voice. Think I'll keep my mouth shut. I want to hear more.*

Someone came in, the other two stopped talking, and the door opened and closed again. Murphy finished as fast as he could and raced into the corridor. Too late, they had disappeared. He walked quickly to his office. "Bring me a roster of the officers assigned to the Army section," he told his master sergeant. "And get my wife on the phone."

~ **Twenty Nine** ~

Ambassador Liu Chen Zhang Li presented himself before Abby in the Blue Room. He wore the same formal suit of stripes and tails and top hat. Both of his hands extended downward alongside the seams of his trousers, military style.

He bowed deeply and spoke softly, "President Steele, the Chinese people send their respects."

"Please convey the sincere respect of the American people to yours. Please." She motioned for him to sit.

Li still reminded Abby of a penguin with his short bows of the head and occasional dip at the waist.

"Mister Ambassador, I need some answers," Abby spoke crisply. "We have discussed this many times. Your country has taken possession of the Spratly Islands, and your armada in the Indian Ocean has diverted oil from its original destination to your own ports. This is dangerous."

"So dangerous that your country sailed an armada from your west coast?" Li's voice had an edge of uncertainty. "The press deems its purpose is to fight our Navy."

Her cheeks reddened. Abby touched her hair and shook her head, "We're sorry the press misconstrued our intent. We deployed them for a simple training exercise near Hawaii."

"Three aircraft carriers?" Li said.

"I know how it must seem, but I assure you we do not want to fight China. But, I need to know, *sir*, does China know this is heading for war?"

"We have only peaceful intentions, but, of course, oil is of vital importance to our nation. And, after all, it was your planes that shot down two of our fighters."

"Not before your planes shot down ours."

"As I've stated before, there is no assurance your plane was shot down by our fighters."

The President pointed to a tape recorder. "You still deny it was your planes. I shouldn't have to convince you, but I'm willing to try. Listen to this. It's from the black box recovered from our plane. The voices are the pilot and his crew."

She pressed the play button. The box emitted a crackling sound, then the first voice.

"Hey, Money. Check your nav — you sure we're only a hundred out from the Spratlys?"

"Roger, checking."

"How far are we from the nearest land?"

"Three hundred miles as the crow flies from Vietnam, about the same from Brunei and Malaysia."

"Like, we *are* the crows. We should be outside fighter range — like, what're those assholes doing here?"

"Shit, Jelly. Shouldn't we have had a heads-up from our AWACS?"

"They didn't come from a land base, unless they were tanked."

"Details, baby. They're here. The Chinese navy's out here. That's all that counts. Better make the call. No tell'n what those assholes'll do."

"Roger. Switching... *(deleted, security)*. Sent. What're you gonna do?"

"Hey... what we were sent out here to do. Check out the fuckin' Spratly Islands."

"Don't think those two agree — Chinese J-10's found us first. They're trying to turn us."

"Fuck'em. Sail on. I'm headin' for the deck. Hang on, baby!"

"Skinhead! That was a missile that just passed us. The bastards let one fly."

"Call it in."

"Roger... *(deleted, security)*. I hope there's some help around. Like a squadron of fighter jocks! Where are they when we need 'em?"

"Hey! We're hit! Hang on, we're go'n in!"

Abby watched the ambassador's eyes. He remained stoic, his expression cold.

"Proof enough, Mr. Li?"

"Merely meaningless tape," he said. "Possible forgery. I do not accept it as proof."

"In that case, sir, this meeting is over. Please convey to your government there will be war if they do not cease interfering with freedom of the seas."

~ ~ ~ ~

After the ambassador left, Abby and her daughter again took up their vigil, sitting in the Oval Office, still waiting for word on Richard.

Betty Porter knocked and entered. She asked if Abby would see Sam. "He said it's about an earlier confidential topic, something to do with a palace coup."

"Anna, you'd better stay, I need you in on this. Betty, send him in."

"Mom, not now. Don't do this now. Wait until we know about Richard."

Abby touched Anna's shoulder. "Thanks, dear, but I have to hear what he has to say."

Sam Tallau burst into the Oval Office like a fast-talking grenade. "Madam President..."

Anna got up and whispered into his ear.

Sam's grin faded to a frown. "I'm sorry, ma'am. I didn't know about your son. I can come back later."

"No, this is very important. I want the news."

"Well, I hesitate to tell you this. But... a persistent rumor says some high-ranking officers have considered some kind of mutiny."

"Didn't you say it came from Dr. Wang? That it's happening in China?"

"No. Plato isn't in this. It's here in our own country."

"When you mentioned this to me earlier, I assumed you meant China."

"Yes, a mutiny, not a coup, which would be an attempt to overthrow you. I misspoke before. The buzz is that they, some of our own officers, will not take your orders, maybe worse."

"A mutiny?"

"You haven't heard anything about it?" Sam asked.

"I heard about some disgruntled comments from, and this is confidential, my son-in-law. But a mutiny? You knew about this? You have any specifics?"

"Ma'am, it's only a rumor, but we heard the FBI might be involved in it and... the Bull. That's why it's on the edge of my radar. Apparently the FBI hasn't cut you in and they should... Maybe..."

"Thanks, Sam. Stay with this and please keep me informed when you have specifics — names, places, intentions. Talk to FBI. Cut them in."

~ ~ ~ ~

As Sam left, Walter Coons entered with a sheaf of papers and laid them in front of Abby. She picked up a pen and, in the process of signing them, the telephone rang in the outer office. Margarite Wellaby came to the door and nodded to Anna, who picked up the president's phone.

"They found him," Anna's choked voice and tears confirmed his death.

"Take me to him." Abby gripped the desk to maintain her composure.

"But, Madam President," Walter said. "We have an e-mail from Plato and a message from Admiral Lawrence. Both need a response. We have drafts, but you should take time to read them, to make sure they're okay."

"My spy and the admiral will have to wait. Bring the messages with you — I'll read them on the plane."

In a way I don't want to go, but I have to. I left my tears on a pillow at the White House, but my soul, my quest for spiritual closure, awaits me. Oh, shit, I sound like a fool drowning in self-pity. I do need to see him one last time before I attend to more matters of state. It's not a question of putting it behind me; loved ones can never be forgotten. Buck is not, and neither would Richard, but coming to terms with the reality that he's really dead can only happen after I actually see him. After all, children are not supposed to die before their parents.

"Richard hadn't driven far in his new BMW," Anna explained. "He made it as far as the small college town of Morgantown, West Virginia, just south of Pittsburgh, across the Pennsylvania state line.

City officials, national media, and Secret Service agents waited outside while she made her last private visit with her dead son. The head of the morgue pulled the rolling table out of its wall cavern. "I'm sorry, Madam President."

She stood in a cold, drab concrete room next to his body. His face, ice-blue. Richard's gentle features reminded her of when he was a baby. She touched his forehead and cheek, then leaned over and kissed his forehead. "I'll do the best I can," she whispered. "Rest, my darling."

She turned and strode straight to her waiting car amid subdued shouts of: "Madam President, do you have a few words for the *Pittsburgh Post Gazette*?" and "I'm with the *Wheeling News*; can you tell us how you feel?"

"Madam President, will you speak to the nation?"

"I'm with the *Morgantown Press*. What can you tell the people of West Virginia?"

Her mind bounced with spurious thoughts. *How does a mother feel? How dare you ask that question. A mother never stops loving her child. Let me grieve my own way, for God's sake.*

With her head bowed, she pushed her aching body toward the car. *I once thought I was interested only in people who want to live. Now I want to know why some don't want to. Let me ache as I've never ached before, even when I lost Buck.*

Anna raced to keep up. "Mother, shall I say anything in behalf of the family — Mother?" Her voice tinted with subdued anxiety.

"Tell them I cannot talk right now, but I will speak tonight from the White House."

Abby watched as Anna and Midget Berry huddled for a moment then Midget passed the President's words to the press.

"My mother grieves in private." Anna's voice lowered. "Very often greater grief is that which is silent." In a stronger tone she finished, "My mother sends her thanks for your courtesy and understanding during this trying time."

Within a half hour, Abby was aboard Marine One, a Sikorsky Sea King, airborne for the return flea-hop from Morgantown to Washington. Aboard the chopper, despite her fog of emotional numbness, she read what Plato sent her. She already knew it had been relayed through one of Sam's trusted agents by way of Taiwan. In the message, Plato reported, "Two factions are competing for the top jobs in the party as well as in the government. One faction sees it as a struggle for oil; the other considers it a fight for hegemony in the whole of Asia. China has used silence as their age-old method of dealing with problems."

For Abby the Chinese music had to sing to the right lyrics, or there could be another world war. She must influence their decision some way.

She opened Blake's short message.

FORCES POSITIONED EAST OF THE PHILIPPINES READY TO STRIKE. INTELLIGENCE SHOWS CHINESE ARMADA IMPEDING INTERNATIONAL FREEDOM OF

THE SEAS BY ENFORCING CERTAIN DISTANCES AROUND THE SPRATLY ISLANDS, STOPPING ALL OIL HIGHWAY SHIPPING. SEVERAL VESSELS ENROUTE JAPAN ALREADY DIVERTED INTO CHINESE PORTS.

Abby sent one last message to the premier of China with copies to the United Nations, ASEAN, NATO, the coalition nations, and to Blake.

RECALL OR DESIST BY MIDNIGHT TONIGHT ALL CHINESE NAVAL FORCES IN THE SOUTH CHINA SEA AND INDIAN OCEAN FROM IMPEDING INTERNATIONAL FREEDOM OF THE SEAS AS REPORTED IN ATTACHED DOCUMENTS.

A copy was hand delivered to the Chinese ambassador in Washington and to her own ambassador in Beijing.

She waited in her office well past the midnight deadline without any response. She went to the Command Center, where she sent a directive to Blake. The message read:

TOP SECRET
OPERATIONAL IMMEDIATE
TO: COMMANDER COALITION FORCES
FROM: POTUS
SUBJECT: CHINESE INCURSION

TAKE NECESSARY ACTION TO ENSURE FREEDOM OF THE SEAS, INCLUDING OFFENSIVE MILITARY ACTION AGAINST CHINESE NAVAL FORCES. FURTHER INSTRUCTIONS AWAIT YOUR SUCCESS.

GOOD LUCK, STEELE

From the Command Center she went to the Oval Office, where she took her seat behind her desk in full view of the waiting television cameras.

"One minute, Madam President," the director said.

Looking more nervous than Abby felt, Anna and Midget watched a TV writer make a slight change in wording on the monitor script. He stepped back. "Done," he said, and nodded to the director.

"Twenty seconds."

"All right, everyone, quiet. Five, four, three, two... Come in on her, now, now, now. You're on, Madam President."

Abby looked up from her desk and smiled to the 300 million Americans.

"Fellow citizens. I have two things to talk to you about tonight. The first — not every president has had to take this country to war, and I hope and pray that I am one of those who will not. However, minutes ago I directed Admiral Blake Lawrence, commander of the Southeast Asian Coalition Action Force, to take necessary military steps to maintain freedom of the seas in that region.

"The concept of 'freedom of the seas' has a long history. Americans first fought for it shortly after the founding of this nation. John Paul Jones came to us from Scotland to fight those who, at the time, would take it from us. Since that time, because we are essentially an island nation, we have been a champion of those rights. Why? Because the oceans are our life's blood. Of course we are not the only nation that relies on that freedom.

"China recently moved naval and air forces into the South China Sea and the Indian Ocean. Those military forces have stopped, searched, and diverted certain ships carrying oil from their original destinations, thus imperiling many smaller nations.

"I have appealed to the leaders of China by asking them to recall or desist by midnight yesterday all Chinese activity impeding international freedom of the seas. They did not respond. Prior to that, I sent numerous appeals through official State Department channels as well as some unofficial channels. The United Nations has also appealed to them as has ASEAN and the European Union. Still no response. It appears they don't understand that all nations on earth are interdependent, national interests overlap. It would seem China is bent on only one thing, preserving her ration of fossil fuel at the expense of all other nations. That explains my actions. I will continue to keep all communication channels with China open. We, as well as the other freedom-loving nations, do not wish to enter into another world war like we experienced twice in the 20th century. However, fellow citizens, Americans have never run from a bully.

"The second thing I wish to tell you this evening relates to my son. I could be criticized for doing so because it could be perceived as political. I assure you that is not my motive. My only son Richard was a medical doctor with the University of Pittsburgh Hospital. I loved him very dearly. Yesterday, he succumbed..." A mix of emotions washed over her. She choked back a tear, dabbed her eyes, and continued. "...to the terrible mental illness called bipolar disorder. He committed suicide. My reason for telling you about this is not to solicit sympathy, but rather for you to hear the news first-hand and not from the evening news. I will shortly announce a new foundation dedicated to seeking a cure for this insidious malady.

"Richard had ideas for a world of the future. Noble ideas. Ideas we all think about but seldom act on. I told him I would do my best to help the world achieve his vision. I will soon announce initiatives that will bring a new beginning for some of earth's problems.

"Like your sons and daughters, Richard was my life and a wonderful man. Despite the sadness this brings to my family, I assure you I remain your president and am fully capable of meeting the challenges of this office. Good night, and may America continue to be blessed."

~ Thirty ~

In the Balabac Straits at 1100 hours, local, October 16th, Blake huddled with his Chief of Staff, Vice Admiral T. B. "Bomber" Joseph, commander of the United States Seventh Fleet, aboard his flag ship, *Lincoln*. A video monitor showed satellite intelligence images in real time, overlaying a chart of the region.

Bomber's shirt collar lay open with its three stars sparkling in the glow of the command console. Many of the 21st century, "over-the-horizon" officers, as Lawrence called them, added a touch of individualism to their uniforms. Bomber wore a kerchief wound loosely around his neck. Some women officers accented their staid Navy blue with a belt of twisted cloth or a bright scarf.

Lawrence acclimated to the new century's culture but, of the old school, his interest lay in not how they dressed but how they fought in combat. Technology might be updated, equipment modified, but American sailors never changed. Quality sailors operating the latest platforms, technology, and weapons systems would always trump quantity.

Small red lights glowed in the darkened room. Sailors moved silently from one combat station to another. Complex techtronics filled an otherwise drably-painted Combat Center. A map of the Spratly Islands flashed on the monitor. It overlaid grids showing five "kill boxes" outlined in red. A lieutenant hit the remote, changing the slide, and rattled through his briefing. He gave radio frequencies, tactical call signs, refueling points, and rescue plans in the event they were shot down.

After listening to the tactical details of the coming action, Bomber and Blake moved to a smaller cubical in the dimly-lit Combat Center and privately reviewed the strategic mission based on the latest intelligence about the capabilities of the opposing force.

The two knew a larger Chinese naval force had moved away from the Spratlys and into the Indian Ocean while a smaller one remained behind, ostensibly to guard the islands they captured. Based on that intelligence, Lawrence positioned a small amphibious force north of the Spratlys and out of range of any Chinese surveillance aircraft. At the same time he moved his battle force, which he named "Sea Freedom," from the Philippine Sea through the Sulu Sea and past the island of Palawan, about 300 miles from the Spratlys. As they passed through the Balabac Straits, he ordered *Eisenhower*, his cat-and-trap carrier, to come into the wind and prepare to launch.

He ordered the amphibious force with the new *Constellation*, one of his two short-deck carriers, to move into position and prepare for an over-the-beach landing by a small force of Marines using their tilt-rotor aircraft.

Lawrence stood on the flag bridge, wind coursing through steel gray hair cut short for sea duty. The strap of his binoculars pressed against a shirt collar with four silver stars, missing the promised fifth still languishing in Congress.

"We're ready to launch, Admiral Lawrence," Bomber said.

"Make it so." His voice contained a quiver of excitement and resonated like a door slamming shut.

Blake's chest swelled as he looked out to see the catapults launch plane after plane flown by men and women in their tender but idealistic years. He remembered those days and still felt the exhilaration of war. He never felt fear, only adrenaline — no pangs of guilt for sending military men off to possible death, for they wanted the excitement. They thrived on the most significant period of their lives, if they lived through it.

~ ~ ~ ~

Strike Fighter Squadron 907, known as Team Warhorse, was one of four fighter squadrons in the *Eisenhower's* air wing. It consisted of twelve strike fighters supported by a crew of more than 225 aviators, ordnance handlers, and technicians. Warhorse was the only squadron using the first-generation strike fighter "Alpha" model, the newest fighter/attack jets in the U.S. Navy.

The pilots of 907 were called the "hotheads" of the air wing due to the intensive training enroute to the conflict. Warhorse squadron led the ship in the number of hours aloft — more than 1,000 in one month.

All of the jets in the squadron carried the names of racehorses: War Emblem, the almost-winner of the 2002 Triple Crown; Traveler, Gen. Robert E. Lee's mount; as well as Black Jack, the riderless Army horse that accompanied John F. Kennedy's coffin.

Among the Warhorses were Commander Leland "Moby" Nevanivich, age 40, and his executive officer, Commander Willard "Iceberg" Greenland, 39, but ten of their 16 pilots were "nuggets," 21- and 22-year olds making their first cruise into battle.

Dressed in green flight suits, they sat on dark blue Naugahyde seats in the pilots' ready room, sipping coffee as details of their mission flashed on a screen in front of them.

"We've been tasked to five areas of interest in the Spratly region," said the pilot leading the brief, a lieutenant — call sign Streamer. "We're first going to look for airplanes, then ships. It's primarily Chinese navy in that area. If we get clearance, we'll go ahead and take 'em out. This is a no-shitter — be cool." Streamer added, "Pack two clips for the pistol, otherwise you're going to have to throw it at 'em."

The pilots donned their G-suits and survival vests. Each packed a survival map in a leg flap and a 9 mm pistol in his flight bag, in case they ended up on the ground.

On the steamy flight deck, Moby climbed into War Emblem. With the canopy closed and lengthy launch preparations underway, the cockpit felt like a sauna. The equatorial heat wrapped around him like a bearskin robe. Flight deck crews hooked the jet to a catapult. Moby saluted, signaling he was ready. The catapult slung the strike/fighter forward at 150 mph and he was aloft.

In the air he met up with Streamer in Black Jack. Together the two planes completed the "strike package" as they flew west.

Moby's sweat-soaked uniform cooled quickly as the jet climbed, and he fought off chills.

Once in Spratly airspace, all jets fell under the control of an AWACS aircraft.

"We've got everybody in the country talking through this net," said Moby. The 'Warhorse' CO spoke into a mask that provided oxygen as well as the mike. "You nuggets know this, but I repeat it anyway. The AWACS's job is to prioritize the most important information and decide who it needs to go to. Everyone else has to shut up."

Moby and his wingman Streamer were just inside the air envelope when the AWACS radioed instructions to forget the anti-air targets.

"We've got some immediate tasking for you — stand by, 907," the controller said.

So what's new? Moby thought. *Seems we never go to the target discussed in the briefing. The* controllers always find targets they like better. It's like when your kids decide they want Denny's — you pull up — they want McDonalds."

"All right, Roger that," he answered the controller.

Moby knew hunting targets from high altitudes could be difficult. Even after reviewing satellite imagery before takeoff, there could be deadly mistakes. *I once refused to fire my weapons when controllers directed me to follow a road and bomb the compound at the end of it. It wasn't obvious from on high, but when I got near the ground, the target turned out to be a hospital.*

When we were briefed, we were told the Sea Freedom Battle Group predicted an easy battle because on paper the amphibious force was superior. But I know better. The job of taking back the Spratlys could quickly become a complex and hazardous campaign. We'll face a number of challenges. Targets are hard to find. Smart bombs aren't always smart — they can fall short or misdirected. The Chinese have been there long enough to establish a strong defensive anti-air system. We'll draw anti-aircraft and shoulder-launched surface-to-air rockets. But the real danger will be from enemy missiles. It'll become a dodge-and-shoot event.

"You don't want to be the first pilot shot down by a Chinese missile," said Moby said to his lip mike. "Firsts are good, but that's not one of them."

"You got that right," came the response from his wingman.

Moby rolled over the target area north of the Spratlys. He looked for his assigned Chinese bunker to destroy. He thought he spotted it and asked the offshore littoral craft to shine a laser beam on the target. As he raced in, War Emblem's spot tracker locked on the laser-marked target. Moby let go one of the 1,000-pound laser-guided bombs from under the jet's wing. It homed in on the spot and exploded in a flash of orange fire. Debris flew into the air mixed with brown smoke and flames.

"That's a shack!" The operative in the boat shouted over the radio, confirming a direct hit.

Finally the Marines gained a foothold. An operative on the ground, a forward air controller, directed the warplanes. Out of concern for civilian casualties, the controller identified two nearby off-limits villages. Then he identified the real targets: Chinese bunkers and heavily-fortified positions holding ammunition and troops. Using a laser, he painted the targets and called the planes in to attack the enemy positions.

During intense anti-aircraft fire, Moby dropped his bomb on the bunker. He saw a string of secondary detonations from exploding ammunition. Then his eye caught an enemy rocket zero on him.

"Bug and run time," he said as he yanked his aircraft into a high-G maneuver. Streamer stayed with him like a fly on glue. At the same time, Moby dropped War Emblem's flares, putting out a heat signature as a decoy for the missiles, and climbed out of range.

The other jets dropped their bombs and followed suit. Mission accomplished.

As they circled, one of the fighters developed an engine problem. Moby ordered Streamer to accompany the jet back to the ship.

The mission stretched the range of the Warhorse jets and the endurance of pilots. But Moby refueled eight times and remained on station to monitor the site. For hours he watched the target through night-vision goggles. All remained quiet as the Marines mopped up.

Finally the AWACS controller told Moby, "Return to base."

"Roger, check'n out."

Carrier missions over the islands lasted six hours, and Moby's 6-foot-3-inch frame sat immobile for hours atop a hard ejection seat. Nevertheless, the toughest job still lay ahead: Landing the jet on a carrier on a black night. Approaching the carrier, he popped a peppermint candy into his dry-as-a-sand-dune mouth. Like other pilots, he didn't worry so much about crashing, only his grade. Every landing is graded, score posted on the ready room wall for peers to see.

~ ~ ~ ~

Back in the ready room, Streamer and the others awaited Moby's return. They knew the skipper would be exhausted after his longer-than-usual flight.

Iceberg, the squadron's second in command, said to a nugget, "No sweat. He'll get back, but it could be close. He's already been in a lot of hostile shit. He's sapped — spent a lot of energy. Now he's got to concentrate. It's all about landing on the boat, baby. Get some rest. I'll call you on his approach."

Some went to the racks, but most killed time watching a "gun camera" video showing the results of an earlier strike on a warehouse. "Kaboom." a pilot said admiringly as the building went sky-high.

At 12:25 a.m. Iceberg alerted his pilots that Moby approached the pattern. The entire squadron gathered around a closed-circuit television to watch and listen to Moby's jet trying to get aboard, catch a wire, and come to rest on the deck.

As he settled to 1200 feet and 250 knots and lowered his gear, he felt two violent jolts and saw two huge flashes in his canopy.

"Hey, War Emblem's falling out of the sky. Passing through 890 feet and 130 knots — lost my HUD."

One of the boys in the ready room turned up the volume on the speaker. They all leaned forward, tense, listening to skipper.

"Airspeed and altitude. Climbing." His voice sounded calm.

"HUD back."

"Can't climb. Up gear — flaps half."

"Slowly climbing — bad yaw," he said.

"5000."

"Declaring emergency. Lost right engine. Clear airspace for me."

"Roger, 907," came the response from the ship.

"Trying right throttle."

"Oops, pop and bang."

"Idle."

"Caution warning RENG STALL."

"Shutting down. Right engine's gone to shit."

The boys in the ready room smiled as they listened to a pro on how to fly a broken airplane.

Iceberg, the squadron XO, ran out of the ready room, and soon the boys heard his voice on the freq with Moby.

"Try a right turn," Iceberg said.

"Negative, left turns only," Moby responded.

"Better check hydraulics," said Iceberg.

"Roger." After a moment, "Hyds okay — can lower my gear. Emergency brakes okay... For our boys who are listening, this is what we've practiced *so* many times in the sim. Don't ever get behind the power curve. One engine can't keep up with it."

"Okay, if you don't get aboard the first time, we're going to have you hit the tanker," Iceberg said.

"Negative. I'm not hanging out over the water with only one engine *any* longer than I have to. I'm getting aboard on *this* pass. baby. If I lose my other engine, I'll have to eject. But get the barricade ready —in case."

For the ready room boys, Moby's voice sounded really smooth — no nerves.

"907, ball, 3.5 single engine."

Iceberg read the NATOPS warning, "Going to afterburner/single-engine on a wave-off with greater-than-on speed AOA (angle of attack) could cause you to go out of control."

"Ball, add a little power." Paddles chimed in.

"Uh-uh. I'm already in AB."

"Po-WER!" Paddles called. "EASY with it."

Bam. Everyone heard it. The boys in the ready room felt the deck shake directly over them.

Moby was into the two-wire for a good safe pass aboard. He sat in the wires, stunned for a second as Paddles and the air boss came over the radio to say, "Good job, skipper."

Moby's hook wouldn't come up, so he had to wait for a tow. He finally got out of the jet, smiled, and said to the maintenance guys, "This bird is *down*. Thanks for the good left engine, but you can have your lemon back."

The deck guys loved it.

When Moby saw Paddles, he said, "Piece of cake."

They gave him the "OK-underline" score. Moby knew it was the grade he deserved — the one reserved only for a really solid landing under dire circumstances. Usually the highest was just an "Okay."

Everyone from the carrier air group commander (CAG) to the admiral congratulated him.

After a classified debriefing, Moby walked into the ready room. His body was hunched and stiff. His face showed exhaustion, but his smile was as wide as the Mississippi River. His team, still waiting, threw up their hands and shouted.

He waved them off. "Nothing. It was nothing. You didn't think the old man would miss a wire and have to bolter, did you? Okay, you bozos. Get some rack time. There's no dwelling on the last mission in our Navy. Remember, there's nothing too difficult for those who don't have to do it. But you have to do it!"

In a 36-hour period, Moby, Streamer, Iceberg, and the rest of the Warhorses would fly another 15 hours. In less than eight hours they were scheduled to brief for the next combat mission.

~ Thirty One ~

Thanksgiving came like a summer day with a fall date. Abby flew to Camp David aboard Marine One — to think, to grieve, and to have a few days of quiet solitude and tranquility before Anna, Murphy, their two boys, and pregnant Third arrived for the holiday.

Abby's feelings were compounded because the week before, Anna had her brother's body moved from the small church in West Virginia to a grave in the Mount Washington Cemetery, high above the south side of Pittsburgh where Richard's father grew up and where Richard lived while attending university. After the burial Abby took her place in a quiet alcove of the local funeral home. Suffering her loss in silence behind a dark veil, she met Richard's friends, some of whom had not known about his illness. They came to meet Abby bearing flowers and said a few words of consolation. Sadness written on their faces, they returned to their lives amid the former mill town turned high-tech heaven.

Abby hibernated. Dressed in faded Levis, a pullover sweater, and tennis shoes, she wrote and conducted business from inside the main cabin.

She tapped a pen against her teeth. How do I deal with China's reckless surge into the Indian Ocean?

She thought about the broader issues of world politics. *People like to think of nations as if they were chess pieces: White or black, good or evil, kings or queens, knights or pawns.*

Her mind rambled through her many travels as Secretary of State, where she met most of the heads of government and all of the foreign ministers. She thought of them as equals, even though some of her own country's leaders thought of them otherwise. In her mind she was constantly aware, although America was today's elephant, sometime in the future it could be a just another cow chip on the world's pastureland. *After all, America is less than 300 years old. Throughout history there have been other great empires, all of which were either destroyed or faded into mediocrity.*

For the first time in history, the people of earth could destroy not just an empire, but the complete planet. Regrettably, war still exists. One misstep with a nuclear bomb could trigger a holocaust, but just as likely the misuse of the earth could cause as much damage. There are obvious resource shortages on the planet, but the solutions are allocation, conservation, and invention — not war. I wonder what the proximate lifespan of earth really is, based on population increases and escalating shortages? Another thousand years? Or is it hundreds? We can't leave it to the next generation, it's our responsibility.

Her warnings to the Chinese government to turn back the naval forces that threatened the petroleum routes had gone unheeded and unanswered. She received a message from Blake. He reported severe resistance, but he regained the Spratly Islands and moved toward a confrontation with the larger Chinese force patrolling the sea-lanes west of Singapore and the Strait of Malacca.

The outcome of our engagement with China is unclear. I pray for a response from the leaders of this most silent and secretive nation. Must we go beyond keeping the sea-lanes free? No! It must be stopped there. We cannot risk another world war. Blake expected more difficulty in the coming sea battle. Techno-edge doesn't guarantee victory at low cost. There will be many casualties.

A chill crept up her spine and across her shoulders. For a moment, her heart pulsed wildly. *Will Blake come back to me?*

To calm her nerves, she opened her journal and wrote:

A fall day. A sad day. A restless day. A thinking day.

I love the sound of silence, the smell of rain.

The colors of the leaves reflect my mood: Some dull brown, some bright red. My worst fears were realized when I lost Richard. Manic depression is such an insidious disorder. Why couldn't I have known earlier? Maybe I could have intervened. Could I have? But how does one recognize it, and even if I had recognized that he was bipolar, would Richard, as an adult and a medical doctor, have done what I asked?

Then there is General Mullin. What a jackass. I hear about him and his back-patting, shoulder-rubbing around Congress. Does he think he can get away with anything he wants? Surely he must know about Article 88 of the Uniform Code of Military Justice? What to do about a seditious general? Do I fire him, bring him up on charges, or peremptorily relieve him? Wasn't it Benjamin Franklin who said, "Everything that one has a right to do is not best done."

In all my time working on the Chinese problem, I have yet to understand them. It must be me. Other national leaders do better, I think. On the other hand, the last report from Sam Talau hinted the Chinese naval force may be operating on its own, carrying out only a sketch of a mission. Could it be that this is a rogue force with no government control, at least until its political leadership is sorted out?

I'm the one charged to get this one right.

She put her pen down and gazed across the pond and into the woods. *Wonder how great-great-granddad Lewis Cass would handle the Chinese? He had to handle the Indians in the Michigan Territory.* My guess is he would say, "First, preserve our nation, then preserve humankind, in that order."

Betty Porter knocked on the door. "Madam President," she said from the other side. "Your family has arrived. They're passing through the gate."

Abby's face lit up like a lamp at midnight. "Wonderful. Get them settled and have them meet me in the family room."

They sat surrounding her, respectful, quiet — almost too quiet. Murphy had his children practically sitting at attention. Abby surmised he gave them a boot-camp kind of lecture before their first visit to the camp.

"Well, are you all settled?" Abby asked after hugging each one and taking her chair at the end of the room. Bear and deer heads hung on the walls and moose antlers over the fireplace, gifts from the Teddy Roosevelt estate.

Silence.

"Answer your grandmother," Murphy growled.

"Murphy, don't sound so West Point," Anna said.

"Anna, I..." Murphy's jaws tightened, obviously wounded by his wife's rebuke in front of Abby.

"Yes, ma'am," Muscle and Bone said almost simultaneously. Their body language reflected the awkwardness they felt visiting their "presidential" grandmother, although their smiles indicated otherwise. Abby had not seen them, except for a few occasions, in more than nine months. It seemed to her the twins had grown bigger and stronger in even that short period of time. Both were strapping 17-year olds with no fat. In today's parlance they were called flat bellies.

On the other hand, Third, sitting next to her brothers, was clearly subdued. Her boyfriend's body language showed he was not overly impressed, and he swaggered when he walked.

197

"Grandma, this is Ralph Newland," Third said.

"How do you do, Madam President, I'm very glad to know you. Your work in the White House is right on target. I'm going to change my first name to 'Dan' or 'Ron'. Ralph is a good name for a businessman but not for an entertainer. I'm finishing at Juilliard, where I'm in training to become an actor and singer."

Abby remained silent as he rattled off too much stuff for a first meeting.

"My father's a Wall Street broker, and my mother's an off-Broadway actress. I'm going to make it as an actor, but if I don't, I can fall back on my father's business. He always wanted me to go to work for him. But I prefer to follow in Mother's footsteps."

Despite sounding overly sure of himself, she was certain underneath he was nervous. *Could it be a touch of New York superiority? She smiled politely. A bit too much puff of his early accomplishments, but what do I know? Maybe he can deliver. On the other hand, it also sounds as if he's touting his worthiness to be living with my granddaughter.*

She changed the subject. "Let me tell you about Camp David. President Franklin Roosevelt established the camp in 1942 as a retreat where he could escape the summer heat of Washington. He called it his 'Shangri-La,' the name of the perfect mountain kingdom in *Lost Horizon*, a famous novel by the English author James Hilton. Eisenhower, a West Pointer, not much into books — sorry, Murphy —

renamed it Camp David for his grandson, David Eisenhower.

"But the best part," she looked at the boys, "the camp has a pitch-and-putt golf course and a swimming pool. There's also equipment for lots of other sports, though no football. Dinner will not be for a few hours, so if you boys would like to go out and play, now is the time."

"Can we, Dad?" Muscle asked.

Murphy nodded his head and added, "Don't get dirty, and be back here on time."

The boys were dressed in clean, pressed trousers, with dress shirts and neckties that Abby knew were seldom worn. Anna nodded and smiled her approval. "Before you go, tell your grandmother about school and what you are up to," she said.

Again Murphy cringed.

"Ah, okay, Mom. Ah, Grandma," Muscle said, "Nothin' much has changed since we saw you. I'm going to the Point next summer. Football season has been good. We have only three games left. Could win the championship. Grades are good. That's all." He looked at Bone, who had his head down, staring at his belt buckle.

"Ah, ah — Grandma, I'm trying to get into the University of Maryland. Good wrestling team. As Harmon said, football is going good. My grades are getting better."

Muscle jabbed his brother in the side and said, "Duh, Cornelius."

"Duh yourself ⸺ Harmon, Harmon, Harmon," Bones said.

"Cornelius, Cornelius, Cornelius."

Murphy came out of his chair and stood in front of his man-size teenagers. "Stop that. You should be proud of your given names. I'm sure..."

Before he could finish his thought, Abby interrupted, "So, they're still running from their names. Well, at Thanksgiving dinner, I'll tell you both about your namesakes and also about the name Anna. Murphy?"

"Yes, ma'am?"

"Won't you let them go out and play?" Abby asked.

"Of course, Madam President."

"Murphy, we're not in the White House. Please call me Abby."

Murphy's face seemed to relax. Whatever bothered him earlier peeled away. He motioned the boys outside and took his seat. "How about Mom instead of Abby?" he grinned for the first time.

"I like that, Murph. Why don't you and Ralph play with the boys while we fix dinner."

"Can I help?" Third asked.

"Didn't know you were a cook, dear," Abby said. "I bet your mother told you that this is the only time they let me in the kitchen ⸺ except to loaf, as I often do in the White House. I don't know why, but I've always liked to cook. Didn't really learn how growing up in Saginaw, but I became interested in it when we visited the Steeles in Pittsburgh. Come along. Anna, Third, you both coming?"

"I think I'll join the boys, Mom," Anna said. "But before we go, Murphy and I need to talk with you in private."

"Go along to the kitchen, Third," Abby said.

Anna waited until the room cleared. "Mom, the reason Murphy and I are out of sorts is because he wants to break the Army's mutiny thing wide open, and I told him not to until we talked to you."

"Do you have more than you did before, Murphy?"

"Not really — the names of several officers, but I know what I heard, and I think it should be stopped immediately. Can't let this thing get out of control."

"Hmm," Abby made her sound. "And, Anna, you told the appropriate persons?"

"Yes."

"Then let's not spoil our Thanksgiving. Let it play out."

~ ~ ~ ~

In the kitchen, the White House cook chopped lettuce for the salad.

"Polly, this is my granddaughter Anna. We call her 'Third.'"

"How do you do, Miss Anna?"

"Please call me Third. Everyone does. So as not to confuse me with my mother and my great-grandmother."

Polly smiled and went back to work.

"Let's see. The turkey is almost ready," Abby said to Third. "Why don't you finish the extra stuffing? I'll do the potatoes."

They worked in silence for several minutes. Finally Third said, "You know about me, Grandma?"

"What's that, dear?"

"I'm pregnant."

"Hmm." Abby thought better of saying anything.

"You can't tell, can you? But I'm already three months."

"Hmm."

"Ralph is the father. He's willing to marry me, but I'm not sure I'm ready."

"Hmm."

"I'm just finishing Barnard. I, ah, I really would like to try something."

"Hmm."

"What do you think, Gran?"

"What do I think? Hmm." She continued to peel the potatoes. "Well, what is your life going to be? Have you mapped it out?"

"Well, I want to be a book editor. And I want to write. And maybe go on to get a master's degree."

"That's a lot. Of course you'll have to do all that with a child. Do you love Ralph?"

"Hmm." Third made her grandmother's sound.

Abby mashed the potatoes, waiting, head down in silence.

"I guess I do. Enough to let him give me a baby."

This time it was Abby who said, "Hmm."

A few seconds of silence.

"Does he love you?" Abby asked.

"He says he does. He's asked me to marry him."

"Hmm."

"Thanks, Grandma," Third said. "You've been a big help."

~   ~   ~   ~

At the Thanksgiving meal in the rustic dining room, surrounded by her family, Abby felt more comfortable than she had for some time. The table itself came from colonial days — a tree trunk cut flat on one side with sturdy wooden legs. Bowls of potatoes, both white and sweet, sat next to hot rolls and cranberry sauce. Murphy sat at the one end of the table with Anna on his right. Third and Ralph sat next to Anna, the boys on the other side with Betty next to Abby.

Abby asked Murphy to say grace, and he responded with a short sentence about missing Richard and their gratefulness to be together on this day.

Following the "amen" and the clank of dishes, Betty piled the boys' plates high and passed on the food. The conversation around the table was less strained than when they had arrived.

"How did the sports go?" Abby asked.

"I won the horseshoe contest," Muscle said.

"Did not," Bone said. "You won one game. Dad and Ralph won the rest."

"Well, at least you didn't win any, duh."

"I should have been out there with you. I was pretty darn good at horseshoes in my day," Abby said. "Could turn them over so they opened up for the pin almost every toss. Next time, if my old bones still let me, I'll take you both on." She passed the platter of turkey. "How long has this displeasure with your given names been going on? Four, five years now? I heard about it, but..."

"It happened about the time they started football in eighth grade," Murphy interrupted. "Someone made fun of Cornelius, and then they did the same thing to Harmon. The kids came home and made up new names. Anna and I went along. Of course, no one makes fun of them now, but the nicknames stuck."

The boys hardly looked up from stuffing their mouths with food.

"Mind your manners," Murphy warned.

They paused for a moment to look at Abby then continued to shovel.

"Well, you should know about both the first Harmon and Cornelius. Do you boys like stories?"

"I guess," Bone said.

"They were quiet, tough men in their time. Harmon was the only son of Lewis Cass the first, who was governor of the Michigan Territory. It was Lewis who brought Michigan to statehood in 1837. It's said that in Harmon's time, according to legend, Paul Bunyan raged among the queen's troops like Samson among the Philistines. They say he had a blue ox that measured 42 axe handles with a plug of chewing tobacco between the horns."

"Ah, Grandma. There was no one named Paul Bunyan," Bone laughed through a mouthful of turkey.

"Was so, duh," Muscle said. "According to my history book, he was a giant lumberjack on the frontier."

"Legendary. Legendary only."

"Well, I like that you challenge. It's good that you do. You don't have to believe your grandmother." Abby shook her fork at the boys. "Look it up. It's in the library. Anyway, the CASS businesses got started as a result of what they called Michigana Fever. Everybody would make a fortune from trees, Green Gold."

Abby ate a fork full of turkey before continuing. "Harmon employed his sons, my great-grandfather

205

Franklin and great-great-uncle Henry, as 'timber cruisers' to scout the Saginaw Valley. The two boys, young and very tough, were also expert judges of pine. A dollar and a quarter an acre bought tracts of land in those days. Next they built the sawmill in 1857, and CASS Lumber was born. Franklin, only 22 years old, chiseled our first log mark with the initials C-A-S-S before floating the trees down the Saginaw River. Uncle Henry, more mechanically inclined than Franklin, developed the gang saw, and pretty soon the machine business got started.

"Now, Cornelius, who lived in Pittsburgh, was your granddad Buck's father. Your mother knew him. All his life he was known simply by 'C.J.' He apparently didn't like the name Cornelius either. He was an Irish mill worker, a minor union leader, a major pub performer, and sometime alderman for the south side of Steel Town. He was a tough mill worker all his life, strong as an ox and very popular. In fact, so popular, Anna the first, also known as Mother Steele, had to send the boys, Buck and his brother Richard, who was killed in *the* war, to the pub to bring Cornelius home. If she didn't, he would spend his entire paycheck buying liquor and beer for the other steelworkers.

"Well, you get the idea. The names in our family are the names of good, tough men, and it's not your fault you have them."

Although quiet all during supper, Anna spoke up. "C.J. was funny and sometimes vulgar, but always a first-class bigot. He refused to come to my wedding."

206

"It isn't that we didn't like our names or disrespected them, it's just that..." Muscle paused.

"What?" Murphy asked sternly.

"Well, ah, the kids said they were nigger names," he mumbled.

"What?" Murphy exclaimed. "Muscle, Bone. Who said that?"

"Well, that's the reason we changed our names. It's the truth, right, Bone?"

Bone still chewing, nodded his head in agreement.

Murphy looked at his wife, then Betty, then Abby, and his daughter.

"Do you mind if I comment?" Betty asked. "I know this is a family discussion, but I know something about the nigger thing. General, do you mind?"

"No, go right ahead, Commander."

Abby sat back. She had never known Betty to intrude.

"You changed your names about five or six years ago. That's not long. You boys remind us the race thing has been a 140-year journey and... America has still not arrived. But in defense of this nation, most other places are way behind." Betty's voice rose, reflecting her passion. "Now, names. Today, there are no 'nigger' names. Not anymore, if there ever were. Our tradition of immigration makes it far easier for the acceptance of any outsiders, whatever their names. Do the names 'Colin Powell' or 'Condoleezza Rice,' or 'Betty Porter,' for that matter, sound like 'nigger' names? The first two were the names of the highest-ranking black people in the George W. Bush administration, and both of them were secretaries of State. Names don't make the person. There, I hope I didn't overstep."

Murphy started it. He clapped, then Abby clapped, then they all exploded and thanked Betty.

"Now that we're talking about our heritage," Abby said, "I want you all to know, before you read about it in the papers, that there may be a family scandal brewing. There is a rumor that challenges my parentage. Pay no attention to it. I am the daughter of Big Lewis Cass and very proud of it."

"So what's a little scandal?" Anna said.

A Secret Service agent approached Abby. "Ma'am, sorry to interrupt, but Secretary Flanagan has asked to speak to you."

"Please excuse me. Betty, thank you. That was wonderful. I'll be right back."

But Abby didn't return. She sent word to the family, "Tell them something important happened and they should enjoy the rest of their stay."

She got into the car, was driven to Marine One, and took off for the White House.

~ **Thirty Two** ~

For Abby, Thanksgiving ended that evening when she landed on the heliport at the south lawn of the White House.

She went directly to the Command Center, the giant technotronic room connected by communications, electronics, and computers to the vast American defense system. Wilmer Flanagan, Reed Alseño, and Plexico Crocket met her. She noticed Mullin's absence, but she didn't ask about it.

"They finally broke their silence," Wilmer blurted. "The new leadership of China, Madam President. They broke their silence!"

"But too late." Alseño shook his head. "Lawrence is already engaged. There's a hell of a war going on in the Indian Ocean as we speak."

"How did they make contact?"

"Who?" Reed asked.

"The new Chinese leadership?"

"Ambassador Li called me," Wilmer stated.

"What was the message?"

"They were distressed about the Spratly Island engagement and were on the verge of declaring war on us. The ambassador did leave some wiggle room, though. He wants to know your reaction."

"Hmm."

The two secretaries stood at her side in silence as she pondered the situation. She gazed at the massive plotting board that showed the Southeast Asian and Indian Ocean regions. Her eyes followed the electronic track of the coalition force, colored in green, and the Chinese force, colored in red. It was not real time but satellite close. Her eyes followed the green line that moved from east of the Philippine Islands, past the Spratly Islands, and then south toward Singapore. Instead of going through the Strait of Malacca, the force split with the major element continuing south on the eastern side of the Indonesian island of Sumatra, through Selat Sunda, the southern passage into the Indian Ocean. A smaller force consisting of one carrier and a few cruisers and destroyers remained just east of Singapore. Ahead of the main group, she saw the tracks of Blake's submarines. He had sent them ahead two to three days earlier. From Selat Sunda, his major force traveled northwest. The projected intercept with the red line was annotated to be at 2400 hours last night.

Reed Alseño broke the silence. "Lawrence advised us the shorter route through the Strait of Malacca was too dangerous, a choke point. The Chinese lay in wait for him and would strike when he was most vulnerable. Instead, he left a small force on the eastern side of Singapore in case the Chinese tried to get back to their home port. Lawrence's main force launched planes before midnight and rockets shortly thereafter. By skirting Indonesia, we believe he caught them off guard.'

"Admiral Crocket, what do you think?" Abby asked.

"The Chinese may have an ace up their sleeve. The Chinese admiral is none other than Pengfei Chen. He's the mastermind of 'Assassins' Mace,' their secret war strategy."

"What does he have out there?" Abby asked.

"What do you mean?" Alseño asked.

"Lawrence's forces."

Plexico Crocket answered. "Four carriers: *Lincoln*, *Eisenhower*, the new *Conny* with its vertical take-off fighters, and the Australian carrier *Perth*, which is also vertical take-off VTOL configured." Defense pointed to Lawrence's order of battle shown on another display board. "He's also got four cruisers, six destroyers, six SSNs, and lots of cruise missiles. Of course, he also has logistics ships and a ready group with a V/STOL configured amphibious carrier and a couple thousand Marines embarked."

"What do the Chinese have?"

Admiral Crocket scratched his head. "Our best intel is based on their transit through the Straits about four months ago, which is a bit suspect. It's from our satellite stuff — a couple of 20,000-ton Brazilian-style CTOL carriers and several 45,000-ton new Chinese short take-off carriers very much like the Soviet Kiev class. The big ones carry about 24 fighter/attack planes."

"CTOL?" Abby asked.

"Catapult take-off and landing, the old cat-and-wire carriers," Alseño answered. "With their new SU-27/J-11 and their J-10 fighters."

"Like the ones our Marines shot down?" Abby asked.

"Exactly," Crocket said. "They also have cruise missiles on submarines, cruisers, and destroyers. This is going to be a no-shitter – excuse me, ma'am — a dog fight and the first real naval battle at sea since World War II. The Chinese have no sea battle experience. We, on the other hand, have had continuous operational work, but we've not been opposed by a blue water force."

"We do have the best admiral in the world in charge of our battle force," Alseño added.

"I'll bet on us," Crocket said. "But we'll have casualties. Lots of them."

A momentary chill ripped across Abby's shoulders at the thought of casualties. She spoke in measured tones. "I wanted to keep this freedom-of-the-seas conflict low, under the radar. I don't want it to rise to the level of a major war. But we're at it, so I guess we'll find out if they found their 'Assassins' Mace'. While Lawrence works on the military problem, it's time for us to work on the political level. Find out what this new leader of China is made of. Wilber, get me the Chinese and Russian ambassadors."

"Tonight?"

"Yes, tonight. It's time to talk."

~ ~ ~ ~

While waiting for the ambassadors to arrive, she contemplated a messy political situation. If I have to fire Bull, I'll merely prepare an explanation to the American people and Congress.

As she read the paper, Sam, dressed like a Wall Street broker, was ushered into the Oval Office. The director of the CIA was always in uniform, his Brooks Brothers suit and red tie. His eyes darted around the room, the signature of his furtive nature.

Following him came FBI Director Donny Freeman whose mashed face matched Sam's — a bent nose, rough complexion. Donny's background was much like Sam's: He'd served in the Marines, got a law degree, and then joined the agency. Donny, a former police officer and lawyer, joined the FBI and rose through the ranks. Spending a lot of time in Washington, he relied on patronage to climb the ladder. Tall and slender with strong shoulders, he looked at his feet, a sign of his embarrassment.

"Please have a seat."

Sam took a chair, but Donny Freeman continued to stand on the Great Seal in the center of the Oval Office rug.

"Sam. What do we have? Is it bad?"

"Not as bad as it could be, ma'am," Sam said. "Director Freeman, do you want to tell her what you told me?"

"Ahem, first I wish to apologize and offer my resignation, ma'am," Donny said.

"That might be in order," She said firmly. "But let me judge for myself."

"Well, ma'am, I learned of a group of military officers who were talking sedition. I did nothing about it. I was wrong. I was not and am not sympathetic to their thoughts, but I frankly didn't think it possible in our country. I thought it would die like it did once before — during President Clinton's administration when officers were openly seditious in their talk." He looked at Sam as if he needed help to explain.

"The two of us put a team on it and traced the whole thing to some of Bull's cronies. I'm not sure he was that much involved, but we *do* know Bull was aware of it and didn't slam the door on it."

"How many are there? How deeply do we have to root?"

Donny opened a notebook and scanned the page.

"Many of the career officers stayed away from the whole thing. But a bunch, in what we call the

214

'redneck' category, jumped in like moths under a lampshade."

"Do we have a list?" Abby asked calmly.

"Yes, ma'am. It's quite extensive with a few very senior people from the Army, but most are just middle grade. I'll make this available immediately," Donny said.

"Okay," Abby said. "What next?"

"We learned there will be a secret meeting of some very senior people tomorrow tonight."

"Will Bull be there?"

"No, he's smarter than that. But he'll have one of his underlings there."

"If he weren't so big, I'd beat the snot out of him!" Abby said to Sam, her face drawn. "Like I need this now?"

"Madam President," Sam offered, "I have my lawyer working on it. Congress needs to be aware of any action you decide to take. You should expect this to make headlines, particularly if you relieve the senior people involved."

"I swore I would protect this house and this office. I shall do that."

~ Thirty Three ~

Despite a fuzzy halo spread around a low-hanging moon in the east, it was darker than most Washington nights.

Dressed in mufti, their collars pulled up, shoulders hunched, heads down, guilty eyes shifting furtively, men left cars parked several blocks from the basement room of their hotel secret meeting place.

Across the street in a truck, parked among a line of cars, four agents and an army officer sat huddled over receivers. Recorders spun their tapes as the crew listened. Others behind bushes watched through infrared devices, and some took photos.

At the door a field grade officer welcomed the figures quietly.

"Evening, colonel," the greeter said to a tall, angular man. "Take a seat or mingle with the others."

The door locked after the last person entered.

A tall, gray-haired man in his late forties moved from a group to the front of the room. "Gentlemen... and ladies, let's get started. Please take a seat."

The room, full of short-haired, military-looking men, also held a few women. They quickly found chairs. Most leaned forward, showing interest in the speaker.

"Boss could not be here." He spoke in choppy sentences. "I'll conduct the meeting. It'll be short."

"Where's Bull?" whispered a man with a crew cut and baby face.

The gray-haired man frowned and spoke in a sharp tone. "Not sure who you are referring to, but that was an inappropriate question." He spread his legs as if at parade rest. His right hand stroked his chin. "This administration is out of control. We have no commander-in-chief. She is a threat to our nation, our way of life. Now, are we in agreement?"

Heads moved up and down, words mumbled.

"Hell, yes."

"You got it, sir."

"Damn right!"

"In my twenty-eight years, I have never seen the armed forces with such low morale. It's on the radio, TV, and is the buzz throughout America."

"She recalled her lover to active duty," one front rower grinned.

"Five stars? Bullshit," another said.

"That's not all," another said. "Everyone knows she threatened the chairman."

"Hell, she stopped the Navy from deploying, then turned around and deployed them herself. She's wacko! Something has to be done. She sure doesn't know what she's doing!"

The gray-haired man interceded in what bordered on a cross-room out-of-control shouting match.

"Enough! We all know the issues. You know this is unprecedented for us to even meet like this. I urge you to speak carefully and go about your business as if we never met. This is not a mutiny. That word can never be spoken ... to anyone. Hear me? But I encourage you to think about the ways you can show your disagreement. One method is to take all your leave in a lump, but at those special times when something is happening. Another, dump addressees off your action messages, very subtly causing confusion on any mission sent over from the West Wing. Of course there is the ultimate method..." His voice drifted to a low mumble.

In the van, they caught only the words "do her" and "volunteers."

"That's enough," said an agent inside the truck. "We should move. Now. Quickly."

"Not so fast," Brigadier General Murphy Perks said. "We have to wait until we have all the evidence. This is bad stuff. The president's lawyers want lots of facts. New ground. Be patient. Keep recording."

"General, you're not in charge here. You're not even supposed to be here."

"I am here at the president's wishes, and I *am* in charge."

"Who breaks it up?" another agent asked.

"No one," Murphy said. "Nothing is to be done without the president's order."

~ **Thirty Four** ~

Margarite Willowby stood like a statue quietly listening to her boss uncharacteristically vent her rage.

"I don't care what he believes. I do have a man I love whom he can neither touch nor criticize. Although I can imagine what they call Blake behind his back — the president's male prostitute, or worse."

With each rant she moved her head up and down. "I suppose Bull's in the same camp as some of the members of Congress who believe the president shouldn't have a man-friend. Then there's my black son-in-law and mixed-blood grandchildren — what a burden for the good ol' boys to carry.

"It's his right to speak his mind, but he stepped way over the line. It's one thing to think about me and all the things he doesn't like, but to permit himself to comment to others and align with officers who threaten our national heritage with mutiny? Stupid! Even the thought of it turns my stomach. Well, bring him on."

"Madam President," Margarite said in her usual quiet manner. "Walter would like you to look at these policy matters." She sat a stack of papers on the President's desk.

Abby read the short one-page notes attached which gave her the pros and cons and a recommended decision. She took their counsel and signed some of the documents others she set aside to add her questions in red ink. Margarite would then take them back to Chief of Staff Walter Coons who would sort, assign, and track each to its final conclusion. Walter, wealthy in his own right, an attorney turned first-class real estate developer, contributed big dollars to her campaign and got the worst job in Washington for his trouble. Nevertheless, he seemed to find the work satisfying. It fit his M.O. of being a behind-the-scenes shaker.

Abby held one paper back, putting the short list for the new chairman of the Joint Chiefs of Staff into her top desk drawer. "I'll talk to Walter privately about this."

Margarite nodded and crossed paths with newly-promoted Captain Betty Porter who knocked then entered. "Madam President, General Mullin is here. He has his lawyer with him. Sam Talau is also waiting. He has Dr. Wang with him."

"Plato. How wonderful." Abby sat back and looked at her hands. "A lawyer. Sounds interesting. But I think I'll see the general alone. We'll call the lawyer later if we need him."

"The lawyer is a she."

"Oh?" The corner of Abby's eyes pinched. It's uncharacteristic for Bull not to hire a male. Must think a female a necessary for politically correct dealings with me.

"Please show in Sam and Dr. Wang. The general and his lawyer can wait."

The two diminutive men entered.

"Welcome back, Plato. You had me worried. We thought the police had you. Not so, obviously."

Plato smiled brightly.

Abby touched her hair, got up from her desk, and came to greet them. "Is it proper for the president to hug a spy? Come here." She was a good foot taller, and when she wrapped her arms around him his nose fit right into her bosom.

"Hmm, very nice." His voice muffled with his head still nestled in her well-covered cleavage.

"Plato." Sam growled. "She's the president."

"It's good you're back. I was worried. Have a seat and tell me where you were and what you learned."

They moved to the couch near her desk. She sat in the nearest chair.

His smile faded. "My condolences, Madame President. I just learned about your son."

"Thank you, Dr. Wang."

His face changed to a less concerned look. "I'll be quick because I know you're busy. In China, an insider sent word the police were looking for me. I stayed with my mother. She's a descendant of the Ming dynasty and has many friends in the Beijing area. My father also had many merchant friends. Between the two groups, I was given sanctuary in homes at various places around the capital city for about a month. I moved every night to a different home. This turned out to be a godsend, because many of these people had high positions. They brought me information about the government from inside the Great Hall of the People. Would you believe they even did *Jesus Christ Superstar* in the hall? This is a Buddhist nation. That's how much things have changed. I had a hard time getting messages to you until I found a way to get information to Taiwan. You received my e-mails?"

Abby studied her hands. "Hmm. Received your e-mails? Yes. Your mother comes from an illustrious family. Ming Dynasty? Isn't that the one that looked down on all things foreign? Are there many descendants of that dynasty?"

"Yes, Madame."

"I remember," she said, "When the first European traders visited China the rulers treated them as inferiors."

"Not the Mings. The Mings were good," Plato said. "My mother knows a dozen or more people in Beijing alone who claim to be descendants. They have meetings and talk about ancient history. It all bores me, but not them."

"Please continue your brief, Plato." Abby smiled at the squat man with the cue ball head. She also wanted to delay as long as possible her meeting with Bull Mullin. In fact, she would have preferred not to meet with him at all.

"There's a power struggle going on in Beijing. A man named Wen Chen vied with his boss, Li Fang, to replace Sun Yuxi as President. The two, Chen and Li Fang, look so much alike that it's difficult to tell them apart. But they're as different as day and night — Wen Chen is ten years younger. The people I talked to think Sun Yuxi likes him. Right now everything is a mess. No one seems in charge except the right-winger Li Fang. We think he's the one who sent the naval force south to take the Spratlys and diverted the Middle East oil to China."

"So that's it. Power. It happens in America, just in different ways." She glanced at Sam. "Plato, you have served the nation very well, and I have something for you. Betty," she called. "Bring it in, please."

The captain left and returned carrying a box. Abby rose. "Dr. Plato Perestrello Wang is hereby awarded the Presidential Medal of Freedom, the highest decoration that we can bestow on a civilian, for intrepid service to the Nation." She took the medal from its box and pinned it on his chest.

Plato looked astonished. He shook her hand, and then bowed deeply. "I don't know what to say. I love this country. This is the greatest honor. Thank you, Madame President. If I can serve you again, just say the word."

~　~　~　~

Eyes hard, lips parted, showing only a touch of teeth; Bull's smile was phony and dishonest. Every strand of his black hair was combed straight back and in place. A bit jowly, his fair-skinned face showed a rubicund shade caused not by fear but by anger.

"Good morning, Madam President," Bull said.

"General Mullin. How good of you to come over from the Pentagon so promptly. Please have a seat. I understand you've been waiting a while. I'm sorry about that." She pointed to a couch. He turned and slid to his place carefully so as not to disturb his freshly-creased uniform with its many rows of ribbons. She strolled to an overstuffed chair. A coffee table separated the two. His posture reflected his unease, hers, erect and confident.

"How are Florence and your family?" she asked. "And how do you like your coffee?"

"Out of the pot, ma'am."

Her friendly demeanor caught Bull off-guard. He inched back in his seat and relaxed a little. His growing paunch pushed against the buttons of his service uniform, causing small openings.

She noted his big, fleshy hands when he picked up the cup and sipped with a large finger extended daintily.

His tobacco-stained teeth parted in a half-smile, and his eyes scanned her as if a trophy, not his President. "My lady's doin' jus' fine, thank you. Miss

MADAM PRESIDENT AND THE ADMIRAL

Florence's got the children out of high school and into college."

"Good. Sounds like they're happy. How are the Redskins doing? I understand you're quite a fan."

"Good team for a change — good coach, new quarterback. Don't miss a game 'less I'm on the road with my duties," he responded.

"Will you stay in the Washington area?"

"You mean when my career is over? Don't know. Family still owns a farm in Macon, but..."

"The papers have been a bit rough on my administration recently, don't you agree, general?"

"You have been the buzz lately, ma'am."

"You know why you're here, general?"

"No, not really."

"Well, we'd better get to it. From the beginning I've hoped we could work as a team, but our relationship has been a bit shaky, wouldn't you agree?"

"I'm mighty sorry about that, ma'am. I never meant no harm."

She wanted to correct him by saying, "any harm," but she overlooked it. It was his country way, he'd probably been saying that since he was a boy, and it endeared him to most people. As a matter of fact, under different circumstances, she probably would have liked him. He came across as an oversized teddy bear, lovable and friendly — on the outside.

"Are you aware we uncovered a group of officers who plotted, of all things, a mutiny?" She shook her head and tucked her chin as if in disbelief. "Or at least some seditious talk?"

"A mutiny?"

"Yes, even an assassination attempt. I don't really know what they had in mind. Maybe to refuse my orders — maybe order the armed forces to do something their civilian superiors did not approve. Have you heard anything about that... no, don't answer. It could be considered entrapment. I wouldn't do that to you. I do respect your service to our country but not your behind-the-scenes politics. We know you have knowledge of this group."

"We?"

"The FBI and CIA."

"I want my lawyer. She's right outside."

"Well, let's look at that. Under Article 88 of the UCMJ, you could be court-martialed. That would cause the country a great deal of harm. This thing can be solved right here in my office, and no one need know the difference."

"You mean?"

"Yes." Her hands came together and she studied them for a moment then looked him in the eyes. "You serve at the pleasure of the president. I would accept your resignation on the promise that you squelch this whole ridiculous thing."

"If I don't?" His face grew very red. His eyes flew back and forth like a caged sparrow.

"I will call Secretary Alseño who, I assume, knows nothing of this yet, and Sam Talau and Donny Freeman, who know everything. I would call for an inquiry to learn who else is involved. So far the evidence is overwhelming. We know their names. We can connect you." She wrinkled her nose. "Messy business. It would hurt the country. You're a patriot, as am I. But you go, one way or another, with or without your lawyer. Your call, general. You know I don't bluff. We go to court, your family gets hurt — and you don't run for office. I want your answer right now."

"Do you know what it takes to become chairman of the Joint Chiefs?" He leaned forward with his arms spread. His big hands shook and moisture welled in the corners of his eyes.

"About as much as it takes to become President of the United States," she answered in a gentle tone.

"You're willing to change the chairman in the midst of a war?"

"You made that decision easy," she said with a hint of a smile.

His eyes changed to defiance. "You know, you're not wearing a crown."

"George Washington passed on that opportunity. He decided that being president was better than being king, but if I did wear a crown, you would be one of the thorns in mine."

She stood and he came to attention.

"I do want your answer, but I also feel sorry for Florence and your children. Take until 8 a.m. tomorrow to submit your resignation. I already have the name of the next chairman on my desk."

~ Thirty Five ~

It was an orange-colored morning in December, the kind found near the Equator when the sun is still low. Blake paced the flag bridge in the warm Indian Ocean wind. His weathered, tanned face framed tired blue eyes that gazed above the billowing clouds spread across Sumatra to the east. A low mist hung off the outer islands.

The Sea Freedom force was about a hundred miles south of the equator, moving rapidly to meet his old acquaintance and now enemy, Admiral Pengfei Chen, in battle.

Seasoned by the changing technologies of the small wars like Korea, Vietnam, Gulf, Afghanistan, Iraq, he prepared to face an enemy with over-the-horizon warfare using cruise missiles from surface ships and submarines, long-range jet bombers, and high-tech communications. *But the real difference will be the determination, training, and experience of thousands of just plain sailors who die in battles for the nation. Napoleon's maxim was, "Every soldier carries a marshal's baton in his knapsack." So it's my turn again. Winter is a good time to fight in the Indian Ocean — the weather is first-rate for war.* His mind spun its review of the coming battle. *I have our forces dispersed around ZZ, the vital area, plus battle space management in place. The submarine, missile, and air threat axis awaits northwest with the winds and currents favorable, west-by-northwest.*

Lawrence raised his binoculars and scanned the horizon, to see every ship in her proper station. He took a drink of black coffee, long since grown cold.

Our destroyers and submarines are in the van with ASW planes searching for subs. V/STOL aircraft are on the small decks as pouncers. The force is dispersed in an anti-missile formation. Our airborne early warning aircraft are along the axis bulged in maximum threat-detection radius. Our fighters are already orbiting. Attack planes are loaded with HARMS, laser-guided Hellfires, and infrared-targeting Mavericks. Our small boys, the cruisers and destroyers, are ready to dance in protection of the big ships, and their boxes are loaded with over-the-horizon missiles.

An officer brought a paper for him to read. He scanned it and handed it back. "Thank you, John. No response needed. Carry on." Then as an afterthought he said, "No, wait. Are our Global Hawks up yet?"

"Climbing out now, admiral. It was tricky getting them airborne, but they're in the sky and they'll soon be there, at altitude, high. They'll give us good intel."

Admiral Lawrence raised his glasses again and looked in the direction of the threat. He reflected on this new addition to reconnaissance. *The Predator unmanned aerial vehicles will certainly help since they can fly up to 40 hours at a stretch and if they get shot down, no men or women are lost.*

I know a lot about our forces but little about theirs. What do I know? They did a manned space flight — Shen Zhou 3. They shot down one of their own satellites. Maybe they can pull the plug on our Global Positioning System and our communications satellites. Our lights would go out, but only temporarily. They have the new FC-1 fighter and the JH-10A fighters. Their V/STOLs have shorter legs than all our planes. Their in-flight refueling is suspect. They have long-range cruise missiles — SS-N-22 Sunburns — a supersonic, sea-skimming anti-surface weapon but they only have a range of about 90 miles. But those are not our main problem. Pengfei Chen is obsessed with finding a secret weapon — the 'Assassins' Mace'. Does he have it? What is it? Lasers? Particle beams? Intelligence-gathering satellites? Some new space technology or a new rocket? How advanced will it be, and can our boys handle it?

My intuition tells me he could use the islands to the east to hide some small craft to launch his Sunburn rockets. Must keep early warning over there.

"Chief of Staff," Lawrence said over his shoulder to Bomber. "I need better intel. What are our satellites getting?"

Bomber shook his head in agreement. "We have ID on every merchant in the Indian Ocean but nothing on the Chinese, sir. It's as if they disappeared. We don't know where they went. Several days ago, their force was two days west of the Nicobar Islands, waiting to launch on us if we came through the straits.

Now they're nowhere. I think we better launch our aircraft now, sir."

"Agree. Get everything we can spare airborne. Let's find them quickly."

He strode off the bridge and into his cabin where he took up his pen and dashed off a short personal note to Abby.

My darling:

It has been several months since you came to see me off to this final adventure of my life. I want you to know I'm grateful for many things. First, for knowing you — and I wish you would change your mind about my ongoing question. Marry me, please. I already miss our dances. Second, for letting me do this one more time. Needless to say, I love the Navy — everything about it except the casualties to good American men and women. Last, for your leadership of this nation.

At this moment, we are on the verge of attacking and being attacked by the Chinese force that has been harassing the sea-lanes. I believe the battle will be brutal, and many American lives lost. Should I die, I want you to know I love you like I have never loved another. If that happens, no matter what anyone else says about you, my basic military mind encourages you to run for another term. You are good for our country. Above all, do what you believe. Do what's right for the people of our nation and humanity. What are we if we are not what we believe?

Remember, there is no shortcut to greatness. Only history will determine if you are the great woman of this time and place.

Lastly, as my grandmother Hildur told me, when you fight a war, make certain it leads to a more peaceful world.

Americans trust you to seek that end.

Love,
Blake

He put down his pen, folded the notepaper, and sealed it in an envelope. On the envelope he wrote, "To be opened only by POTUS." He put it on his desktop where it might be found easily and lay down on his bed. As he dozed off, a knock came on his door.

"Yes?"

"Admiral, it's me, Bomber."

Blake swung his feet to the floor and sat up. "Come in."

Bomber entered with the intelligence specialist, Commander Gardner Jeffords, a lanky man with unruly hair. "We've got some strange information, admiral. It seems our satellites show several oil tankers with unusually large electronic blips. We think the Chinese use them as shields. Satellite radar tells us their ships piggyback — one naval ship with one merchant."

"Hmm. That's not new — right out of war college gaming. I thought he'd be more original than that." Lawrence rubbed his eyes. "We should confirm this. Get a Global Hawk over there. We must not damage or sink any civilian ships if we can help it. Our forces must have positive identification. Do we have aircraft in the vicinity? Let's send them in for a look also. I'm moving into the Combat Center. Come along... Have we sent a warning to all merchant ships and civilian aircraft to avoid this region?"

"Yes, sir. Went out about two hours ago."

"Then we should see some merchant movement soon."

Lawrence took his seat in the Combat Center of his command ship, a vast war room filled with a techno-ganglia-cyber communications and radars. Some naval officers in the modern Navy argued that combat commanders need not go to sea. They believed naval wars could be fought from a building ashore using satellite and battle-transmitted intelligence. But Admiral Lawrence felt the commander must always be with the fight.

His chair sat high in front of a chart of the Indian Ocean projected on a vertical screen. Electronic tracks displayed friendly ships and aircraft so the admiral and his staff could monitor the real-time activities of the force. His staff surrounded him, passing information from time to time, but otherwise waiting for his orders.

Lawrence's mind converted it to an old-fashioned tabletop as if he looked down from the heavens.

"We should have made contact with the Chinese by now. They've been warned through the State Department to stop interdicting merchants on the trade routes."

A sailor sitting at a radar/computer console screamed, "Bogie, bearing 347 degrees true. Vampires bearing 340 degrees. Incoming attack planes and missiles, admiral. The AWACS have declared them hostile and our fighters engaged but... man, lots of them."

Lawrence turned to his Chief of Staff. "Execute Operation Sea Freedom. Go hot. Weapons free. Sink the bastards. Hold the nukes."

"Aye aye, sir," Bomber said, then pressed the button that released preformatted flash messages that ratcheted the battle from a hunt and chase to a full-blown exchange of modern, over-the-horizon high-tech weapons.

Lawrence heard the sound of the Lincoln's Phalanx close-in weapon system — mini-guns rattling at a rate of 4,500 rounds a minute — and knew cruise missiles were inbound.

A Chinese cruise missile at wave-top elevation was the first to hit one of Lawrence's destroyers. The ship's mini-guns were ineffective against the surprise attack.

"Strike Fighter Squadron 907 is over that dense bunch of merchants. They report the tankers are no longer following the trade route — seems they've scattered and are running in all directions. The Chinese navy is exposed, and 907 is attacking, sir."

"Do we have targeting?" Lawrence asked.

"The picture is maturing. The Chinese have separation. Yes, sir. We have good target data."

"After 907's attack, clear the strike aircraft and launch the surface-to-surface stuff... What's good for the goose... "

"Warhorse reports a direct hit on a Chinese carrier," an operation specialist said.

"Any casualties?" Admiral Lawrence asked.

"Yes, sir. Squadron 907 already lost three planes. We also have a report that one of the Marine force's defense V/STOLs is down."

"Who?"

"Only names we have are Moby and a new short-deck replacement, call sign Pipes."

Lawrence's weary eyes, now sunk like drill bits, pinched. A hand dragged across the moisture that seeped into his eyes as he recalled the pair decorated by Abby. The moment evaporated.

He addressed Bomber, "Turn the Sea Freedom group to the west, away from the islands. Pengfei is tricky. He has some small craft out here somewhere. Keep an eye on those small islands to the east."

"Aye, aye, sir."

"Target area clear. Squadron 907 headed home to rearm. Two carriers on fire. Many small boys dead in the water. Three more of our planes lost," came a report.

"Birds away." A young operation specialist shouted. "*Shiloh, Bunker Hill, Chosin, Lake Erie* just launched their Tomahawks, sir. There's more: *Kinkaid* and *Benfold* and *Fletcher*. Paul Hamilton reports their birds are off the rail also — it's gonna rain bullets on those fuc'n assho... sorry... Chinese, sir."

"That's okay, son. I've heard it before," Blake said with a smile.

"Yeah, admiral." The sailor's voice sounded hyper. "Everybody eats shit from time to time. It's just a matter of degree, and now they're gonna eat ours, sir."

At that moment, Lawrence's command ship shook violently. The sound of exploding weapons filled the usually quiet Command Center. A bulkhead burst at one end of the room, sending a large ball of fire across the space. Another explosion tore open the bulkhead near Lawrence, knocking him to the floor.

~ ~ ~ ~

In the Blue Room, mid-December, Abby spoke quietly but firmly to the Chinese ambassador. Her secretaries of State and Defense sat mutely.

Ambassador Liu Chen Zhang Li listened.

237

"Thank you for coming, Ambassador Li. I'll get right to the matter at hand. I have been told by Secretary Flanagan your government considers a declaration of war because of the recent action at the Spratly Islands related to ensuring freedom of the seas. As inhabitants of this planet, I know we can be so much better than we are. But *is* your government telling me they are willing to fight Russia at the same time it fights a world war with America and its allies? This is not about oil or hegemony, but about a civil society, a civilized planet, sir. We gave you fair warning to stop interdicting oil traffic. Your nation would not even respond to us, maybe because of your government's political turmoil in selecting a new premier. But, I suggest you *do not* make the same mistake twice. We don't want a world war, but if *you* do, you'll get it. I am the President of the United States, and I'm willing to talk. As you know, a battle is being fought with many casualties somewhere in the Indian Ocean." She paused briefly. "I am confident that when it is over, you will no longer have a navy. I cannot stop the battle, but you and I can stop a much larger war. I reiterate: I am willing to talk. I want you to make contact with your leaders and tell them what I have said. I want an answer within the hour. And keep in mind: I do have some influence with the Russians."

~ ~ ~ ~

Lawrence struggled to rise but fell back. Blood streamed from his right leg, shoulder and neck.

Bomber grabbed a telephone cord and wrapped it tight around the remnant of his leg. Using a heavy pointer as a lever, he applied a tourniquet. "Get a corpsman up here right away. The admiral's hit."

Lawrence felt the searing pain and instinctively grabbed the leg. His hand came up bloody. He shook his head to clear his mind then shouted, "Bomber, get me to an operational monitor. I can still fight this battle. What's the damage to *Lincoln*?"

"We're still in the fight, sir, but your leg and shoulder, sir."

"Keep the tourniquet on the leg. I can make it." He struggled to gain his balance on one leg, but his wounded shoulder lacked the strength to hold him. With his left hand, he grasped a chair and faced the fire burning near an exit door. A damage control team fought the flames with extinguishers.

Through the smoke, a sailor with a bag strapped to his shoulder walked toward Blake. "Let me see that, admiral. I'm a corpsman. Your face's pale — lost some blood. Here, lie down so I can treat your wound. Looks clean. Christ, where's the rest of your fucking leg?"

A sailor in the damage control party threw what looked like a bundle of bloody rags in front of the corpsman. "Here."

Lawrence wrenched himself away from the corpsman. "Don't worry about that. Help me get to a monitor. This fight isn't over yet."

"Bullshit, admiral, you got to get to sick bay, sir. The doc might be able to save this."

"No time. Here, let me see what's going on — I need a picture." Lawrence pushed a sailor out of his way to see his monitor. He shook his head once, twice. His eyes grayed for a moment. He hit a button and the screen changed to the largest scale. He could see the ships and airplanes and the entire battle. To the east near the islands he saw on the radar Pengfie's small boats and incoming Sunburns.

"Bomber? Bomber? Where are you?" He looked around. His eyes grayed again. All at once he felt sleepy, yet he gave a groggy order. "It's the islands — his 'Assassins' Mace' — the Sunburns. Take out their satellite. Launch remaining Tomahawks, the Harpoons... Launch all carrier attack planes. Attack. Attack. The islands..."

~ **Thirty Six** ~

About every hour Betty Porter, accompanied by the Command Center duty officer brought Abby battle summary reports. This morning, Abby took a sip of the steaming coffee and glanced at the first line of the first daily report.

LINCOLN ON FIRE, FLIGHT DECK DOWN

"*Lincoln*? My God, *Lincoln*. That's Blake's flagship." Her heart jumped. A tingling sensation crept up her arm, much like the way she felt when her son was in danger. *Could I lose two men I love so much?*

She forced herself to read on.

SHILOH ALSO HIT BUT LAUNCHED EIGHT TOMAHAWK CRUISE MISSILES, BATTLE DAMAGE ASSESSMENT UNKNOWN; FLETCHER LAUNCHED EIGHT HARPOON MISSILES, BATTLE DAMAGE ASSESSMENT UNKNOWN; AIRCRAFT FROM PERTH PUNISHING THE CHINESE FORCE, REARMING CONSTELLATION'S PLANES.

ELEVEN CHINESE SHIPS SUNK OR SEVERELY DAMAGED. CREWS ABANDONING SHIP. TWENTY-TWO CHINESE AIRCRAFT SHOT DOWN. ONE 20-TON CARRIER AND THEIR TWO 45,000-TON CARRIERS HIT ON FLIGHT DECK; UNABLE TO LAUNCH — RESULT 20 MORE PLANES DISABLED ON DECK.

Abby immediately called for Secretaries Flanagan and Alseño plus the newly appointed chairman of the

Joint Chiefs, Admiral Plexico Crocket, to join her for breakfast. She asked Anna to include Murphy.

In less than a half hour, they sat about a table set with coffee cakes, fruit, and pitchers of hot coffee.

Clearly agitated she said, "The reports show we're beating the hell out of them. Why no response from the Chinese? I should think we would have something from the new regime in Beijing. Even our own Congress doesn't take this long... "

"Look at this," Wilmer said interrupting Abby as he handed her a note. "The Chinese ambassador just got back to me."

Abby took it, gave it a quick glance, then passed the note to Anna, who chewed the last bite of her eggs benedict. She skimmed it quickly and passed it to Murphy. "It states the new premier is willing to meet with you in Beijing. At last they're willing to talk, Mom."

"Those supercilious bastards," Abby bellowed. "Is this really the way they are? Damn it. I'm trying hard to understand the Chinese mind, but just when I think I've got it, I get a new challenge. He expects me to go to his city to negotiate? It's bullshit. Excuse me, Murphy. I don't use profanity very often, but some days... I guess I should chalk it off to time differences and arrogance."

"I'm somewhat familiar with soldier talk, Madam President," Murphy said.

"And look at this," Abby showed the headline of the *Detroit News*. She held up the paper. "Romeo Seward sent this over this morning. The scandalizing bastards. In the middle of a war yet."

WHO IS PRESIDENT STEELE'S REAL FATHER?

What won't they stoop to?" Anna said. "You are really the buzz now. Everyone has an opinion."

"What a day." Abby picked up her coffee cup but didn't drink. She held it by both hands just a few inches from her mouth. "Get a grip," she said. "Right in the middle of a war, they drag out every old saw."

"Don't let this stuff become an issue, Mom. You have bigger fish to fry," Anna said.

"True," Wilmer said.

"True," Abby agreed. "What I should do is counter the Chinese note with a dictum that we will meet in Washington or not at all. Maybe I should just let it be handled by State, not meet at this level. What would you do, Murphy? Should I go?"

Murphy put down his fork and wiped his mouth with his napkin: "Well, Madam President. We... us folk have had a lot of experience with arrogance. Here's what most of us do. We ask ourselves, what do we want? Once that question is answered, the rest comes easy. We've learned to focus on the goal and to hell with things like ego and superior/inferior feelings. As far as the talking heads — they smell a weakness like dogs after a wounded fox."

"I want peace," Abby said. "Our country wants peace. But not at any price. We know it works. Clinton met with Yeltsin nine times — more than any other president. Of course it was after the Cold War years. He closed the gap between Russia and the United States. Personal meetings do work. It's the art of engagement."

"Maybe," Plexico Crocket spoke up, "maybe you want a neutral site. That might work to everyone's advantage."

Betty Porter knocked, entered, but remained near the door as if she didn't want to intrude. She coughed lightly; a frown spread across her forehead. A Marine brigadier standing behind her shuffled his feet.

Abby waved for Betty to come in.

The two visitors approached and stood quietly for a minute. Betty finally bent over, touched the president's shoulder in an intimate gesture, and whispered something into Abby's ear.

President Steele gave her a false smile, put down her cup, and stood. She walked to the window. She resisted the tears forming in the corners of her eyes — her chest heaved, and her shoulders and upper body shook for a moment. She felt the same shimmer up her left arm.

Anna went to her mother and placed a hand on her shoulder. "Mom, you okay?"

Abby shook her head.

"What?" Anna asked.

"Blake is wounded. He might not live." The words choked from her mouth.

Anna, Betty, and Murphy exchanged looks.

"Where is he?" Anna asked.

"In a hospital in Singapore," Betty answered, "ready to transfer to our naval hospital in Yokohama when he's able. It's not good. He's lost a lot of blood. He's critical."

"I need to go to him. But I can't," Abby said. "Damn the Chinese."

Murphy rose and went to the President. Abby, Anna, and Murphy stood with their arms wrapped around each other. No one said anything for several moments.

Finally, Murphy whispered, "Mom, why not set the meeting in Singapore?"

Abby's head turned. Her face brightened for a second. She turned to Secretary Flanagan. "Wilmer, tell them I will meet with the Chinese premier in Singapore. I'm leaving immediately."

~ ~ ~ ~

"How many hours did you say?" Abby asked the airman assigned as liaison between the pilot of Air Force One and the president. The plane made only one short stop in Hawaii for fuel. Abby didn't get off. Instead, the usual dignitaries and senior military officers came aboard to pay their respects. In less than an hour they were airborne again, high over the Pacific Ocean.

"Thirteen, ma'am. We should be there in six more hours."

"Thank you."

Abby turned to Anna. "And you wondered, back at the Pickle Factory, why I needed you with me. People think I'm brave, but I'm not. I'm afraid for Blake."

"You are *so* brave — about everything except the people you love. I know you're more Thatcher than you like to think."

"Any late news? Is he improving?"

"The doctors only say he's still on the critical list. There were many wounded and killed on both sides."

"Is the battle over?" Abby asked.

"All but the wrapping up. Several ships are being towed to port. The wounded are still being flown to hospitals," Betty Porter said. "We've even sent our ships to help with the Chinese survivors."

"Now isn't that the American way? Beat them up, then help them to their feet."

"Now, about these negotiations. What must I know about the Chinese mind?" Abby asked. "Mr. Ph.D. Plato Wang, talk to me."

"Yes, madame. Let me see..." Plato scratched his shiny bald head. "What about the Chinese do you need to know in order to negotiate with them? Well, they are not easy to deal with — you've got to know them. For them, human equals character equals thoughtful conviction."

She listened, but Blake was in her thoughts. *I've already lost three men I cared for: Father, Buck, and Richard and now maybe Blake. I wish this damn plane would go faster.*

"They like sageliness within and, in your case, queenliness without," Plato continued. "They believe in humanism — people come first. They believe in spirituality coupled with ethical character. But don't cross them."

Abby shook her head, "You're telling me more than I want to hear. Keep it simple."

Plato shrugged his shoulders. "I'll try, but it isn't simple. When negotiating, above all, I suggest appealing to the concept of the 'superior man': The man or woman who can make the way great — not the way that can make the man great. For your information, I didn't make that up. It is the most celebrated saying of Confucius."

"Hmm, not an easy task."

"Yes, ma'am. No one has more human experience and skills than you, at least no one I know."

"Let's see. What do we want? Wilmer? Plato?" she said to Secretary Flanagan.

Wilmer, whose mind always worked in logical sequence, rattled off the list. "One, no mass war; Two, do not let this broaden into a global conflict; Three, resolve the resource problem; Four, resolve the

Russia/China border dispute at least enough to open the pipeline; Five, oil exploration and more of it, as well as alternatives to fossil fuels."

"And last: Let them save face." Plato added.

~ ~ ~ ~

Air Force One landed on the sun-baked asphalt of the military side of Singapore International Airport. Whisked away among a line of limousines, she arrived at the hospital where Singapore soldiers, as well as her own guards, surrounded her. The elevator took her quickly to the third floor.

"He's in a coma," a surgeon said. "And very critical."

"You must not stay long, Madam President," said the head of the hospital, a small slender Asian man. "We must monitor him constantly. He lost his leg and may lose his right arm."

"There are no others with wounds as severe as his who survived. He was almost triaged. Except for his rank he would have been," said a Navy captain still in a soiled uniform. "Here, ma'am." he handed her an envelope with her name on it. "This was found in his cabin. For you."

She took the letter. "Will he know I'm here?"

"I doubt it. Nothing has awakened him so far," the doctor responded. "His vital signs are weak. Be careful with him."

Abby walked to the door and peered in. Tears came but she choked them back. She took several big sucks of breath. Blake's complexion matched the bare room, the bedclothes with white sheets and a gray pillow. She went in and stood by his bed. Reaching out, she touched his face then took his hand. She stood there for several minutes looking at his ashen face — the drawn skin of a combat officer. His breathing was sporadic and labored. *What is he thinking? Is he thinking anything? Is he reliving the battle, his long life? Does he hear anything, know anything? What really goes on inside a warrior? They never talk about it — just live their experiences, not like others, who share all.*

She opened the letter and read the note. This time she let the tears flow. Her feelings went deep — a wound that crept through her body and settled in her throat. *I do love him. Does it take a war for me to realize how much? Please let him live,* she thought, lifting her eyes to heaven.

Then she bent over and whispered into his ear, "Darling. It's me, Abby. I do love you. I want you to live so we can marry. Come back to Washington so we can grow old together."

She kissed him on the forehead, leaving a teardrop on the pillowcase.

Abby backed away, dabbed her eyes, and stood for another minute at the door before joining the others.

"Sometimes I believe the whole sky is full of care and concern," she said to those gathered. "This is one of those times. Thank you all for what you are doing." She looked up through the ceiling again and said aloud to an unknown being, "Please let him live."

She turned and walked swiftly to the exit. She couldn't wait to face the bastards who did this. "Instead of talking, I ought to beat the shit out of them."

~ **Thirty Seven** ~

The main Singapore government house stood on the island's highest point, the most historical site. The building's architecture captured a sense of the struggle and many changes of the island's culture. Beginning as a fishing village, it became a British colony in 1819, was occupied by the Japanese during the Second World War, then gained independence in 1965.

Wooden steps led to a large room with many windows but no air conditioning on this hot Christmas Day. Heeding Plato's words, Abby did not make the new Chinese premier suffer the embarrassment of entering the room first. Instead, they would enter simultaneously.

Face, she thought. *Do I care? For progress' sake, let them save it.*

The two sides took their places at a long, uncovered teak table. Young women in traditional Malaysian dress placed teacups on saucers adjacent to each chair. Abby, with her negotiating team left and right, sat across from the premier of China and his entourage. Dr. Plato Perestrello Wang sat at Abby's immediate left to translate for her. His mastery of all the Chinese dialects made him superior to any professional interpreter in the State Department.

Before undertaking the first item of the preliminary agenda, which turned out to be more posturing among staffs, the two leaders politely exchanged shook hands and exchanged mundane pleasantries.

While waiting for the tea to be poured, Abby searched the countenance of her opponent, President Wen Chen, the winner of the political power struggle in China. He did look much like pictures she had seen of Li Fang, the man who lost everything, even his job as premier.

Regardless of how he got to the top rung, Abby thought, *he has the same awesome responsibilities I do, but for a country with almost five times as many people. His domestic problems far surmount mine. On the other hand, I represent the wide international interests of the coalition, and I have to report to a world waiting for good news. Not withstanding the terrible carnage of the sea battle and my feelings about Blake, we do have the responsibility to put Humpty Dumpty together again.*

Abby remained silent; beads of perspiration lined her forehead. She casually sipped her tea to allow the Chinese leader to save face by making the first move.

They occasionally looked at each other across a table lined on both sides with underlings. *He's sizing me up,* she thought.

President Chen made a slight cough. "I know about your admiral, and we hope he survives. We have many dead."

Plato translated. When he was finished, Abby nodded her head in agreement. "As many as fifteen hundred — needlessly," she said, her voice firm.

"We demand reparations," Chen said.

Abby did not respond to Plato's translation, nodding her head to acknowledge that she heard, all the while studying her opponent. *His opening statement is uncharacteristically direct.*

"We can attack you across the Pacific," President Chen said.

Abby then cleared her voice, set down her teacup down, and examined her hands. She did not smile as she looked across the table at the slight man wearing glasses. In a quiet tone, with hardened eyes, she said, "You'll get no reparations." She let her words sink in, then continued. "Yes, I realize your country can attack us across the ocean..."

She paused while Plato listened and confirmed their translation was correct. Her eyes remained fixed on her opponent and drew on all she learned about China's military capabilities. "Your current ICBM force — about 20, are CSS-4 silo-based missiles that *can* reach targets in the United States such as Alaska or Seattle. They consist of large, liquid-propellant missiles armed with single nuclear warheads. You also have about a dozen CSS-3 ICBMs as well as a few medium-range SLBMs. You are concerned about the survivability of your strategic deterrent; therefore, you have entered into a modernization program to develop mobile, solid-propellant ICBMs. But that cannot become a reality until well after 2020. Your country has three new mobile solid-propellant strategic missiles in development — the road-mobile CSS-X-10 ICBM, also called the DF-31, which is now in the flight-test stage. Also in development is a longer-range version of the DF-31, as well as the JL-2 SLBM."

Abby took a long sip of tea to let the information she rattled off settle in his mind. She searched his eyes for the blink. *Not yet*, she thought. "For many years, you had the capability to develop and deploy a MIRV, multiple reentry vehicle system. You could even develop a multiple RV system for the CSS-4 ICBM, but in a few years. Your pursuit of a multiple RV capability for your mobile ICBMs and SLBMs could encounter significant technical hurdles and would be very costly. Shall I go on?"

She saw it. The slight change in his eyes revealed he knew she knew as much, if not more, than he about the Chinese rocket capabilities.

Following a period of silence, one of the Chen's aides whispered into his ear.

He tugged his glasses then spoke rapidly. "Before the talks continue, I suggest we adjourn to let our staffs review existing policies and preliminary national positions."

I made him blink and put him on the defensive.

"I agree, Mr. Chen," Abby countered. "But before that happens, let us hold a private meeting, just the two of us."

Caught off guard again, Chen nodded his willingness — he could not do otherwise without losing face. Both rose and stood at their chairs while the two leaders left the large conference room and escorted to a smaller room.

The sound of rain beat a staccato on the roof. Separated from the larger meeting place, this room held only a small table and several straight-backed chairs. The interpreters sat between them.

The window shutters were closed but the rain continued. Temperatures rose in the small, humid room.

Sweat poured off Abby's forehead and cheeks. "Mr. Chen, the purpose of our meeting is to avoid escalation. America is an abstaining superpower." She waited until Plato confirmed Chen's linguist translated the sentence correctly before continuing. "We do not wish to tell others what to do." She continued as Plato nodded again, "We aspire only to attain a higher moral superiority. Power is the feeling that a nation or a person wants to control people — make them do anything they otherwise might not do. We have the forces to do anything, but we don't want to. Do you realize what you have done to the world economy by interrupting freedom of the seas? China is not the only nation that needs oil. Japan depends on the Middle East for 60 percent, Europe for 35 percent and

America to a lesser extent. As I see it, India and China are ancient civilizations trying to become modern. Are you understanding me?"

She waited for the interpreter to respond.

"He says he understands you, Madame President," Plato said.

"Your people want what they see on TV and in the movies. This situation in the Indian Ocean could lead to a clash of civilizations that we don't want. We want to help you, but your solutions are within your own reach. It seems you need a better method of changing leadership so that the military doesn't get out of control. When the negotiations are over, let us be able to say that we reached for more lofty goals — those that make for a better world. We should ask ourselves, what *will* this century be about? More mass wars or peace? What about life on this planet? Can we contribute to its extension or its extinction? Anything less would be madness. "Abby extended her hands, palms up. "This may seem strange, but one of the ways you can do that is to let your women use their brains."

Wen Chen, who remained quiet and stoic throughout her remarks, bowed politely and stood. She stood also.

"You are a woman of exceptional capacity. I sense you have studied the great Buddha." He smiled, "Are you *sure* you are not him reborn? The next Buddha could be a woman, you know." He smiled and bowed again. "The world cannot be remade in a day, but we can try."

On their return to the main room, both leaders listened to translations of scripted material. Abby's mind remained focused on the negotiating elements and blanked out her thoughts of Blake's condition.

Each side laid out a list of problems facing a peaceful settlement.

"Our side," the Chen said, "wishes to limit the agenda. We would agree to the opening of the oil seaway, sharing the oil fields of the Spratly Islands, resolving the Russian/Chinese boundary dispute, and opening the Pan-Asian pipeline."

"Sir, we can agree to deal with those issues, but it's not enough," Abby said in a demanding tone. "We wish to expand the agenda to include cessation of sea-lane interference and Taiwan's status. We also wish to discuss taking other problems to the world table, such as alternate technologies, pace of industrialization, energy consumption, and human community expansion including population control for China, India, and Indonesia."

Premier Wen Chen thought for a long moment. Then, after discussing with his leading staffer, he agreed to the additions. A wide-ranging agenda was agreed to which would take three to five days to draw up.

Abby had a last-minute session with her negotiating team. Then, with an umbrella held over her head, she made her way to her car and went directly to the hospital.

Blake's doctors told her he seemed to have some awareness of his surroundings, evidenced by a slight change in his eyes.

"If he survives," the lead physician stated, "he'll need a prosthetic on his lower right leg below the knee. The good news, we saved the right arm. It finally has circulation."

Abby asked that a bed be placed in the room alongside Blake's. They agreed.

For the next five days she attended every negotiating meeting and slept every night in Blake's hospital room.

Sitting next to Blake each evening, she held his hand and gently caressed his brow with wet cloths brought by nurses. When alone, she whispered encouraging words. "Darling can you hear me? You will get well, I know it. I need you."

When the nurses came, she helped change his dressings but stood out of the way when it required more complicated techniques. Position papers, brought by her staff, were read between her evening duties to Blake and the few hours of rest she permitted herself.

Negotiations came to an end seemingly too quickly. She and Premier Wen Chen were sped to a joint press conference where both made perfunctory speeches and shook hands.

The Chinese agreed to refrain from interrupting the sea-lanes and to take their resource problem to the United Nations. Abby made no promises about Taiwan. The United States and its allies agreed to make an appeal to Russia to return the disputed portion of the territory north of the pipeline and to restore the flow of oil to China.

The two sides further agreed to work together to develop alternate technologies, such as hydrogen cells and geothermal sources, and to search for ways to curtail the pace of industrialization. Both sides saved face and avoided a broader conflict.

After the first press conference, Abby rushed to the hospital. Blake's condition still had not improved. She was not permitted to see him because she learned he now had little resistance to disease and had contracted both a staph infection and pneumonia.

"There's nothing more we can do but pray," the doctor said.

Dissatisfied, Abby refused to give in to pessimistic thoughts. "Find a way," she demanded angrily.

~ **Thirty Eight** ~

New Years Day came and went all over the world, but Abby was still in Singapore with Blake.

She already knew the answer but asked her staff, "Can I continue to do my job from such a faraway place as Singapore?"

"No, ma'am. The president can go on short trips but should not stay overseas. There is too much pressing business at home: Bills to sign, policies to decide, and money to raise."

She made one last visit. Smells of iodine and disinfectants filled the air.

"Madam President, you should not go near him. It's a critical period. The risk of further infection..."

"Knowing I'm still here," she interrupted, "might be just the right medicine to continue his fight. True?"

"Well, maybe, but..."

"I'll take that chance."

Dressed in a gray hospital gown and wearing a white face mask, she stood holding his hand. "Darling," she whispered. "I'm still here. Please get strong — don't leave me."

She thought, *It may be wishful thinking, but I saw a bit of color come to his face*. She agonized over her decision. *Should I stay with the man I love or do my duties to the nation come first?* She leaned down and whispered in his ear, "I must return home, but I will be back as soon as I can, darling." She kissed his forehead.

At the door she asked the doctor, "Wouldn't he better off in an American hospital?"

"Transporting him would be dangerous, but no more dangerous than staying here. The biggest problem is the staph infection. We worry this hospital is not properly sanitized. Our hospital in Yokohama would be better."

"What would you need?"

"A sanitized aircraft equipped for medical evacuation with the best-trained personnel," he answered.

"How long would it take to get him ready?"

"Late this afternoon," the slightly-built officer said.

"Instead of going home," she told her staff. "I will stay with Admiral Lawrence, but in Japan where I have access to better embassy communications and facilities."

Attendants wheeled him aboard the waiting aircraft on a special gurney. Plastic tubes and white-clothed medical people surrounded him. They took their places in the Army plane specially prepared for the trip.

Abby assisted and supervised so the wheels of government didn't get in the way. On the other end, the government of Japan cleared the path for his speedy transportation to the naval hospital.

Despite the objections of the Secret Service and several high-ranking military officers, she elected to fly in the same plane with Blake. Air Force One, along with several fighters, flew in close formation as protection.

On arrival, Abby called a hasty meeting with the media. "To the citizens of Japan and to my fellow Americans, I am grateful to the government of Japan for making these facilities available for Admiral Lawrence's best chance of recovery. As you know, he was severely wounded in battle, and I feel it is my duty to remain near him. I assure my countrymen I am able to continue my service even though I am overseas. I have excellent communications. May our Maker be with you all and especially the admiral."

Over the next few days, between her duties of state, Abby, or Anna when the president was too busy, stayed at the hospital. Abby summoned her personal doctor, Ellen Wood, to oversee and ensure good care for him. Blake's status seemed to stabilize. The doctors cleared the staph infection but still monitored his pneumonia. He was on a ventilator, and the doctors hoped the antibiotics would do their job.

The news arrived the third day. Anna entered and stood to one side. Abby was holding a meeting by teleconference with key members of Congress about a bill concerning highway improvements that needed a few more votes to pass. She looked up and read her daughter's face. The president took a deep breath and smiled. "You have good news."

"Yes, Mom. He's back. Blake woke up about six hours ago. The fever has broken and he's out of the coma. They say he's grouchy and wants to get back to his command."

Abby looked at the men and women on her telescreen and let out a deep breath. She closed her eyes and a slight smile spread across her lips. "I've just learned Admiral Lawrence will survive. This conference is hereby adjourned."

The people on the telescreen all rose as one, clapped, and murmured their best wishes. Abby went directly to the hospital. After a short delay, Ellen Woods came to her.

"How is he?" Abby asked anxiously,

Her voice sounded raspy and tired. "He's recovering very well. Every doctor here agrees, ma'am: It's miraculous!"

Abby's eyes watered as she sensed relief.

"Is he well enough to travel?"

"Maybe one more day."

"Please thank everyone on my behalf, doctor. May I talk to him?"

"Yes, let me take you to his room."

Her stomach quivered when she heard Blake say, "Is that you, POTUS?"

"Yes — Admiral Lawrence — darling. Oh, Blake! It's so good to hear your voice. How do you feel?"

263

"Good enough to go back to sea. By the way, how did we do? Did we have many casualties? What about Pengfei Chen? Is he all right?"

"Your Sea Freedom force beat the snot out of them. Oil tankers are moving as before, and freedom of the seas is back on track in the Indian Ocean. I'm afraid Admiral Pengfei did not survive. We lost a lot of our own good men and women."

"Oh." Sadness came to his eyes and he shook his head in agreement. "Our people fought bravely. Pengfei was a gallant opponent."

"Blake," she said.

"Yes?"

"I have your letter."

"I know. You told me."

"When?"

"You whispered to me in the hospital. I heard you. I just couldn't respond."

"Then you know what I said?"

"Yes, every word of it. You said you would marry me. You can't back down now. There's no changing your mind."

"Oh, darling. I will. Come back with me, quickly. As soon as the doctors say it is safe for you to travel, of course."

"Are you sure you want to be a Jane Eyre?"

"A Jane Eyre?"

"The book *Jane Eyre* by Charlotte Brontë. Don't you remember?"

Abby marveled that his mind worked so clearly and fresh after a coma.

"Well," she said, "I think I read it while a student at Barnard about fifty years ago."

"Read the last chapter," he said. "By the way, I love you."

"I love you too, Blake."

~ ~ ~ ~

As soon as she could, Abby asked Margarite to find a copy of *Jane Eyre.*

In the quiet of her apartment, she quickly skimmed a book. The plot and characters came back to her. Brontë had developed masterfully a rebellious female who, for Abby, became a model for her own life. Long forgotten in the ruffles of her day-to-day living, Abby felt quite surprised that Blake, a blue-water, battle-tested naval officer, would find interest in the book. Nevertheless, after familiarizing herself again with the very ambitious and much convoluted plot, she flipped the pages to the last chapter and read:

"I have now been married ten years. I know what it is to live entirely for and with what I love best on earth. I hold myself supremely blest — blest beyond what language can express; because I am my husband's life as fully as he is mine. No woman was ever nearer to her mate than I am; ever more absolutely bone of his flesh and flesh of his flesh. I know no weariness of my Edward's society: He knows none of mine; any more than we each do of the pulsation of the heart that beats in our separate bosoms; consequently, we are ever together. To be together is for us to be at once free as in solitude, as gay as in company. We talk, I believe, all day long; to talk to each other is but a more animated and an audible thinking. All my confidence is bestowed on him, all his confidence is devoted to me; we are precisely suited in character — perfect concord is the result.

Mr. Rochester continued to be blind the first two years of our union: Perhaps it was that circumstance that drew us so very near — that knit us so very close: For I was then his vision, as I am still his right hand."

Abby put the book down. She knew the remainder of the story. Mr. Rochester regained his sight in one eye, and they lived out their lives together. Abby thought, *I'm somewhat like the Jane Eyre character, but not for the same reasons Blake alluded to, caring for a crippled man. Rather, the idea of finding love again at my age. I particularly like the part that reads, "blest — blest beyond what language can express."*

266

~ **Thirty Nine** ~

The next summer they chose the main chapel of the United States Naval Academy for their marriage. Annapolis was the school on the Severn River where Admiral Lawrence had graduated and been commissioned more than forty years earlier. Abby's two strapping grandsons, somewhat embarrassed, led the procession and carried bouquets of roses. Immediately in front of the bride came Anna and Mr. and Mrs. Ralph Newland, holding Abby's first great-grandchild.

Abby, her auburn hair worn especially for Blake in a Spanish-style bun, under a small veil, entered through the huge bronze doors where the inscribed motto in Latin said, "Not for self, but for country." Wearing a beige suit with a single strand of pearls, to the traditional tune of "Here Comes the Bride," she walked down the aisle on the arm of Brigadier General Murphy Perks.

Blake's children also came to the wedding. Blake Lawrence IV and his sister Martha followed the procession and took their places with the Steele children in the front row of the chapel.

As she walked, Abby nodded and smiled to friends in the pews then glanced up at the stained glass window portraying Sir Galahad, the symbol of the highest, most noble motive of military service. Light shone through the window onto a simple altar that represented the sailors' sacrifices. She felt proud the country had men like Blake, Murphy, Sam, and Plato.

Ahead she saw Blake waiting at the altar. He wore his white full-dress uniform. Draped about his neck was the Medal of Honor, the highest military decoration bestowed by Congress. His shoulder boards showed the markings of a five-star admiral, also given by a grateful nation. Next to him stood Blake's best man, his Annapolis roommate, Sam Talau.

Anna, the maid of honor, stood to the left side of the altar. Third stood next to her mother, Murphy next to Sam.

Blake smiled at her as she stepped to his side.

The chaplain held a small book in his hands and read, "Dear friends, we are gathered here today to join two of our most worthy citizens in matrimony — a woman who has admirably led this nation and one of our bravest military heroes. Before we conduct the ceremony, let us pray for them."

The crying of Third's infant interrupted the quiet. Everyone laughed, and the chaplain proceeded with the liturgy of marriage. Abby smiled continuously, her eyes never straying from Blake's. He in turn held her hands and transmitted the electricity of his love through a deeply penetrating look into her eyes.

When it was over, Blake kissed Abby, then tried to disguise his limp as they strolled down the aisle among smiling well-wishers toward the steps leading to Chapel Walk. As they passed under the upraised swords of naval officers who had fought alongside Blake, a mass of reporters bombarded them with shouted questions:

"Anything for the people, Madam President?"

"How do you feel?"

"Where will you honeymoon?"

"How about a few remarks?"

"How do you feel about being first gentleman, Admiral Lawrence?"

"Will you run for a second term?"

Will your name be President Lawrence or Steele?"

Their limousine waited at the curb, but before getting in, Abby turned and faced the cameras. "My thanks to all of you. I feel the love of our people — thank you, Americans. We will honeymoon in Madrid, Paris, and Saginaw, followed by a few days on a yacht." She paused. "This may seem a strange time to talk politics, but I've been asked if I intend to run for a second term, and the answer is yes. There is a great deal more work to do. The founders of this nation had lofty expectations."

She didn't want to spoil her wedding day with a major political speech on the steps of the chapel. Yet she had something to say.

"During America's short history we have struggled with major issues and have overcome them. The expansion into the west by my Michigan forefathers and other brave Americans was a major undertaking, but we accomplished it. Slavery was too big to solve — it took a civil war — but we solved it. Equal rights for women and blacks was too big to solve, but we did it. Now the question is, what is the lifespan of earth? Truth will emerge from our democracy to solve the question of our day. Is it time to serve? And to what extent? Can we bring a more human face to the world?"

She added, her blue eyes fixed lovingly at her new husband, "Admiral Lawrence and I intend to examine these new issues. Thanks again for coming."

"Madam President! Madam President! Why the honeymoon in Madrid and Paris?"

"Because we first met in Madrid forty years ago and meant to meet again in Paris for our second date, but missed it.

Author's Biography

Carl Nelson's career as a working writer has spanned more than twenty-five years. During that time he has published seven works of non-fiction, three novels, and more than fifty short stories, articles, and technical papers. His work can be seen on his website www.carl-a-nelson.com

He is a member of the Authors Guild of America, PEN USA, and has twice served as President of the San Diego Writers/Editors Guild.

Carl is listed in *Who's Who in California, 1989; Who's Who in America, 2006; Who's Who in American Education, 2006;* and *Who's Who in the World, 2007.* He is a graduate of United States Naval Academy at Annapolis and holds a Master of Science degree in economics/ systems analysis. His doctorate, earned at Aliant/USIU, is in international business (finance and trade), and he is a professor of international business at the California School of International Management (CSIM) where he has been awarded that school's Distinguished Educator Award.

In his first career Carl rose from recruit to decorated U.S. Navy captain. During a 33-year career he served four tours of duty in the Vietnam War, many demanding staff positions, and commanded five combat organizations. His sea commands included a guided missile cruiser, a frigate, and a fleet salvage ship. His ground commands were as senior advisor to the commander of combat riverine operations in the Rung Sat Special Zone (RSSZ) and Naval Logistics Base, Nha Be.